Winter

Lightning

Book Three: Symphony
A Novel by
Natasha Simmons

Winter Lightning

Cover art by: Anthony Taylor

Winter Lightning

ISBN-13: 978-0-9967127-6-7

Published by Thomas Publishing

Thomas | Publishing

Acknowledgements

Thank you to my dear friend Traci Tucker for always being so willing to read my drafts. Phil Mayes, you have no idea how much you've helped me along the way. Thank you for your input and encouragement. Thank you Amy Hill for being another set of eyes. Thank you to all my fans who happily wander in this world that I have lovingly created. I hope you enjoy *Winter Lightning* as much as I enjoyed writing it. And to my friend Kenny, it may have taken me a while, but I keep my promises.

Happy endings are a matter of perspective.

N.S.

Winter Lightning

*Winter lightning is unexpected bolts slicing through
the frigid darkness.
Who knew it could also happen in summer.*

*I saw winter lightning once.
It was in a dream of a dream.
It thrilled and frightened me all at once and I
wondered if I'd ever see it again.
Rare, brilliant, thrilling—
Like a crack in the sky.
I remember wondering if I stepped through it, would I
find out all the secrets of the world.
Would it know mine?*

Akiko Ishido

Chapter 1

They were dead.

Her parents were dead.

She stood like stone pressed in the tiny hidden space of their sleeping area—her heartbeat reverberating in her ears. When she heard the screams of her mother, she couldn't help herself. She slid the door open a sliver. She knew her father would be very angry with her, but she had to see what was going on. Two men she'd never seen before stood in front of the only two people she had in the world. Both held a gun. Before she could take another breath, gunshots exploded in her ears.

She wanted to scream, to run, to do something besides look unblinking, and choking on the wail lodged in her throat, while the scene on the other side of the door unfolded. Her mother and father clutching each other, crumpled hard on the worn mats they'd prayed on every night for her sixteen years of life—both had a gunshot to the head.

The men left quickly. She stood rooted to the spot. The tremor started slowly as it climbed from the depths of somewhere unnamed, like an awakening volcano on the verge of destroying everything in its vicinity. Then slowly, the scream scratched and clawed a jagged path on its way up her throat, forcing her mouth open wide.

The sound.

The tortured sound that escaped her—she knew she would never forget that sound for as long as she lived. It filled her head, the room, and their home, but was cut into nothing against the chaos of the crowded pachinko parlor below.

Ricco tried to shake herself free from the memories that lived just on the edges of her consciousness. The horrible images took residence in her dreams. They didn't always come to the surface, but they were always there—forever waiting to erupt her world.

She knew why the images of her parents had visited this particular night.

Naricco Maki hated to admit that it was indeed her big idea to do something they'd never done. She figured that since they were in Boston, so far from home during a bakery convention, they deserved a bit of fun.

"Let's do something we've never done," she'd said. *"It'll be fun,"* she'd said.

Ricco wished she'd picked something else like stabbing her eyes out with a fork, instead of sending drinks to a couple of strangers who turned out to be a guy who was not a stranger at all to her boss, Symphony, and a man with eyes like lightning who could seemingly peer into her soul.

It was that man, in part, who was keeping her awake now, and she needed to be up at an ungodly hour as usual to prepare samples for an event in the morning—which was only a few hours away.

The whole damn idea had blown up in her face. They were having such a good time talking, drinking, and had even ordered dinner. The evening was perfect until she'd made a total idiot out of herself.

She hated that her past had a way of snaking its way into her present.

Would she ever escape the utter despair of having absolutely no place to go—no place to call home, and no family. For seventeen days after the tragic death of her parents, Ricco had become quite creative at pretending everything was fine.

Tears pushed from the corners of her eyes, and the pain that grated her heart caused her to grab her chest beneath the covers of the hotel room bedding. A scream lodged itself there. She squeezed her eyes shut and curled into a ball until the feeling passed.

There were thirteen thousand three hundred twenty seconds before she had to get up. She could see the numbers filling her head. She tried to gather the seconds into minutes and the minutes into hours, but she couldn't. The seconds ticked away and grew behind her eyes, pushing at her forehead. She tried to take deep breaths and meditate to push the numbers away. She couldn't open her eyes because there would be so many things to count and her mind wouldn't be able to stop the hundreds of ways they could be calculated.

Most times she could keep this affliction of hers at bay, but when her guard was down, the numbers tried to choke her. Her head was beginning to throb. She inhaled and exhaled in steady beats.

In one, out two, in one…

A chime from her phone made her jump. Her heart raced from being startled back to the present. She removed the covers from her head and felt for the phone on the nightstand. She first noticed it was well past midnight, then she noticed she'd received a text from a number she did not know.

"I wanted to make sure you were ok…"

Who in the world?

Symphony was the first person that came to mind, but Symphony's number was programmed into her phone, so that couldn't be her. It couldn't be him…could it? Could Kenny have texted her? How could he, she hadn't given him her phone number. He also hadn't asked.

Needing to know, she texted, "Who is this?" She saw the dots indicating that someone was texting back.

"Kenny."

Her heartbeats came faster. How did he get her number? Did Symphony give it to him? She must have, but why would Symphony do that? Before she could reply, the dots came again. "I hope I didn't wake you."

Her fingers moved over the keys before she had time to think. "No, I can't sleep." She typed back.

"May I see you?"

Those four words abruptly halted her breath.

No longer caring how he'd gotten her number, she knew that this was much better than her demons waiting for her under the covers. Even if he was a complete stranger. Well...not a *complete* stranger; they'd had drinks and dinner. "Ok...When?"

"Now, if that's OK. May I come up?"

Not once did she worry about her safety or question why she was allowing a near stranger to come up to her hotel room. She simply typed in, "I'm in room 414."

"I'm on my way." came the immediate reply.

Ricco tossed the phone to the side and flew out of the bed. She ran to her suitcase, threw aside the short black leather skirt and white top she'd worn earlier and found some leggings and a top to throw on. She ran to the bathroom, grabbed her brush and tried to bring order to her long, black hair. She heard a soft knock on her door, took another look in the mirror, and pulled all of her hair to the front of her right shoulder. Smiled at the mirror and quickly rolled her eyes at herself.

What the hell am I doing?

Ricco placed both hands flat on the door, looked through the peephole, and took a deep breath.

There he was.

Straight out of a gothic novel.

Electric silver piercing eyes, silver streaks taking over his raven locks, with the face of a Greek god. The hair did not take away from his youthful figure and looks—it intensified the perfection of his features. The man was head-turning, heart-stopping, and apparently hotel-door-opening-to-a-stranger, capital G-gorgeous!

He looked her dead in the eyes through the peephole and she quickly removed her eye.

Again, she didn't question why she was letting this man into her hotel room, but she removed the deadbolt from the door and swung it open.

"Hi." She said.

"Hi." He replied, taking her all in. She wondered what he saw. She felt small, fragile, and insufficient.

Another few beats passed before she said, "Come in."

She led him to the sitting area and they both sat on the sofa.

"I just wanted to see for myself that you were OK."

"Why?"

The question came out before she could pull it back. However, he didn't seem put off by the question or surprised that she'd asked it.

"Because you were so upset."

She'd gotten visibly upset when Terry talked about gentrification and people sometimes ending up on the streets. The subject had absolutely nothing to do with her, yet she'd excused herself and left right after.

She tried to brush off her reaction at the table. "I don't know what came over me. I know I was being silly." She said to him.

Kenny took her hand in his and held her eyes. The combination could truly be her undoing. "Naricco, you don't have to pretend everything is fine with me."

Why?

She wondered quietly in her head, but the answer was plain—it was simple. He could see through her. That realization should scare the hell out of her, but it didn't.

"I don't, do I?"

She was lost.

He leaned forward. She hesitated for three seconds—the numbers pushing their way to the surface. She leaned in slightly. One second passed before Kenny pulled her onto his lap and captured her mouth with his.

She was struck.

The volt of pleasure disintegrated the numbers that had taken root in her mind only moments ago and the pleasure of his kiss rumbled like thunder through her. Or was it she who caused the sound of thunder?

They sat and kissed like that for what seemed like hours. All her senses were alive and pulsing. Kenny Cavanaugh was an instant addiction and she didn't give a damn. She didn't want the moment to end. She wanted to stay lost in the high that was him.

Somewhere from clouds of passion, she heard him ask. "Better?"

Her head resting in the crook of his neck and shoulder she found some clarity to answer, "Are you saying that your kisses were the balm I needed?"

"No. I only intended to offer you my company."

"I enjoyed the kisses as well."

"So did I." He leaned back and kissed her forehead. "Do you want to talk about it?"

She shook her head. She didn't want the awful memories to rise again. "You were right, I just needed the company."

He separated them for a few moments while he grabbed a blanket off the bed. He sat next to her and pulled her back into his arms. She wanted to tell him to go, that she needed to go to bed, that she didn't know him well enough for this kind of intimacy, but she didn't say a word. She needed this peace. She let him pull her back on his lap. He made himself comfortable, pulled the blanket over the both of them. "Take comfort in knowing that you don't have to be alone tonight."

Her throat tightened and she could feel the tears pressing against her eyes. She didn't question how he'd known her greatest fear. She just took comfort in knowing that her heart was light, her mind was free, and for the first time in a very long time, she felt at ease and unafraid.

He held her like that and she slept in his arms free from dreams to torment her. Ricco slept at peace. When her alarm went off, she found herself in her bed alone. For a moment she wondered if she'd dreamt Kenny had been in her hotel room, but the text messages on her phone confirmed that what felt like a dream was actually reality.

She wondered if she would see him again.

Could she see him again?

If she was being honest with herself, she definitely wanted to see him again.

Chapter 2

More than a year later.

"See Kyle, I knew we should've left Friday. If the flight is delayed again, we may miss the grand opening."

"Symphony, may I remind you that it was your idea to go to Marley's birthday party, Saturday afternoon."

"Oh, shut up. You know she's Cadence's best friend. We couldn't miss the party. Especially since Marley came to hers just a couple weeks ago."

"Cadence is two. As long as Foo and Zoo is on the TV, her world keeps turning. The only people Cadence was excited to see were her Godparents. Alexandra and Joshua always do way too much. I can't believe they flew out with so many gifts. Plus, it's your place, you can delay the grand opening if you want."

Two years.

Symphony Dean bounced her daughter on her lap. She could tell she was about to get fussy. Had it only been two years ago when she awoke from a coma with no memory of the existence of the two people who were now her entire world?

Symphony's life had changed so much in such a short amount of time. Before the baby, she'd handed over some of her duties at the bakery to her business partner, Ian. She'd partnered with Ian, giving him a small percentage of the business, because she needed him. She couldn't run Symphony's like it needed to be run, without him.

Since then, she'd let her best friend, Alexandra Phoenix, talk her into opening a second bakery in a newly revitalized area in Boston. Symphony wanted to be part of the rebirth of the neighborhood. There were too many neighborhoods like it that either died or were taken over by developers who weren't interested in revitalizing, but rather rebranding the neighborhood into a more affluent area that would no longer be recognizable nor affordable by the current residents.

She'd met the people in some of the other shops near hers, and loved them. She and Kyle had no plans on living in Boston long-term, but had a townhouse in the same building where Ricco would be living while she ran the bakery. It was not only convenient, but it was also a requirement to live in the neighborhood as well. Symphony and her husband Kyle owned both places. Ricco leased a condo from them.

Naricco Maki, Symphony's golden girl. Since the original Symphony's made its debut, Naricco, or Ricco as everyone called her, had been Symphony's early morning prep girl, but when Symphony was forced to attend a bakers' conference at the last minute when Ian flew off to get married, Symphony found out what an asset Ricco really was. A simple chat over drinks revealed that she was a math wizard and quite the accomplished baker, in her own right. Everything fell into place to offer Ricco the chance to run the new bakery in Boston.

"Symphony?"

"Huh?"

"You OK, sweetheart?"

Symphony looked at her husband. She'd been so distracted, thinking about how much her life had changed. His vivid blue eyes still had the ability to make her heart flutter. She'd met him in this very airport nearly three years ago. His floppy blonde hair and those eyes of his had annoyed her to no end. "Yes, I'm fine." Recently, he'd started wearing his hair much shorter, but he still looked like a gorgeous god of the surf.

"I said, it's your place, you can delay the opening if you want."

"I can't do that. All the advertising, all the food, deliveries, and prep work, none of that can be delayed. Ricco and the rest of the staff have worked day and night trying to get ready. Plus, it's the last week of school, heading into celebration season. It is the perfect time to open."

"You've worked pretty hard yourself. And to be honest, I'm ready for the grand opening to be over so I can have my wife home more often." He reached for their daughter. "Don't get me wrong, I am uber proud of you, but you've been flying back and forth between Jacksonville and Boston for over a year."

Symphony rolled her eyes at her husband. "You've been with me most of those times. Plus, you said you loved the place in Boston." She knew that he'd originally been disgruntled about having to get a place there as a stipulation of having a business in the neighborhood.

"I know, but I still like to have you at home." Kyle waggled his brows with a sneaky smile and placed emphasis on the word "have."

With another eye-roll, she stood, "I'm going to check the status of our flight. Me and Cadence are getting cranky and it's getting late. The opening is in less than twelve hours."

Winter Lightning

At one time, Symphony's life was consumed with running her bakery. For weeks, up until the moment she unlocked the doors, she'd thought of nothing else but her success as a business owner. With the opening of the second Symphony's several states away, it would be easy to assume that she'd be just as anxious. However, she found that a baby and a husband tended to put things into perspective.

Yes, she wanted to get to the opening of her new store, but watching her kid enjoy her friend's birthday party was worth the sacrifice of leaving a couple days later. It had taken Symphony a very long time to let love lead the way and to allow people into her small circle. She'd worked for years with Ian and Ricco and found out just how little she knew them when her store manager, Ian, announced he was getting married in his home town in Hawaii. It gave her an opportunity to find out more about Ian when she made him a partner, but when he'd left for his wedding and honeymoon, she'd gotten a chance to work with Ricco more closely. Now, she and Ricco were the best of friends.

Symphony sat next to her husband again and reached for Cadence. The baby was content to stay with her father who was singing her a silly song. When the toddler became more interested in the little bow on her shoe, Kyle turned to Symphony.

"What did they say?"

"They still don't know when we'll be able to leave."

"We'll get there in time, sweetheart."

"I just remember how stressed I was the night before I opened the store in St. Augustine. I know Ricco; I'm pretty sure she's still there trying to make sure everything's perfect." Symphony shook her head, exasperated. "What was I thinking? I should've flown up there at the beginning of the week?"

"You know Ricco. I know she has everything under control. Her work is her life."

"Yea, that's what I'm afraid of."

"What do you mean? I thought that's why she was the perfect person to run the shop."

"She is, but she also needs to have some fun, find a romance, something."

"I thought you told me she had a thing for Kenny" He'd hung out with Cavanaugh quite a bit and liked the man. He always seemed to be a bit mysterious, but other than that, he seemed cool enough.

"Yes, Kenny. I don't think that worked out. She won't talk about it." Symphony reached for Cadence

22

again, and she came to her that time. "I'm just glad Kenny had nothing to do with starting those fires."

Symphony played the peek-a-boo game with Cadence for a few moments before she realized Kyle hadn't responded. She looked up at him. "What?"

"It's still been bothering me. Why would someone make it seem as if Cavanaugh was deliberately setting those fires? The whole thing seems like it goes deeper than what the investigation unearthed."

She frowned. "Ethan nor Landon would have partnered with him if they thought he was anything but trustworthy."

Ethan Powers and Landon Phoenix were brothers and were in charge of the revitalization project.

"I just think there's more to Kenny Cavanaugh than what he's presenting on the surface."

Some current shop owners in the revitalized area were approached, supposedly by a representative of Cavanaugh Construction, to buy their businesses. The representative was offering two or three times what they were worth. When a dry-cleaning business refused, a week later her business was set on fire. The fire chief confirmed arson, but there was no physical evidence linking Cavanaugh Construction and Kenny was adamant that his company had not been involved. He also had not authorized anyone to approach business owners.

Symphony had no idea that her husband still had questions about Kenny or his company. She'd met him when she and Ricco were in Boston for a bakery convention. Cavanaugh had been with Terry Phoenix, of all people, her former college boyfriend. She hadn't met the rest of the Phoenix men until her aunt passed away. It just so happened that Terry's aunt and uncle shared an island off the coast of South Carolina with Symphony's aunt.

She'd met Landon, Ethan, Joshua, and their wives when her aunt died, but had gotten to know them like family when they assisted in rescuing Kyle's parents and Cadence when they were kidnapped by a man out to exact revenge against Symphony.

Symphony thought about Kenny and wondered what happened between him and Ricco. There'd been an instant attraction, but as far as she knew, nothing had come of it.

"You've gotten quiet on me." Kyle said, quietly.

"Just thinking."

"If you're so worried about her, give Ricco a call. I'm surprised she hadn't called you. Since we should have been there by now."

Symphony pulled out her phone and called her friend. She sighed heavily when there was no answer.

"I guess. She's busy or isn't near her phone." Before she could try calling the shop, they were finally called to board their flight.

Somehow undetectable by the alarms and systems in place, fire climbed silently up the back wall. Its silent black weapon filled the bakery set for its grand opening the next morning and ascended the stairs to the office above it. Smoke quickly filled the space, choking everything in its path. An exhausted Ricco never woke from where she'd fallen asleep on her desk in the office.

Chapter 3

"Is this where all the work-a-holics meet?" Terry Phoenix asked as he and Kenny Cavanaugh approached Terry's cousins seated at a table in Cliques. Cliques was one of the sports bars owned by Joshua's wife, Alexandra. There was the one in Boston and another in New Orleans. Kenny thought it odd that a lawyer would have a couple of sports bars. He found out that not only did she own the sports bars with her former boss in New Orleans, but she'd been one of the best trick bartenders in the city.

Joshua, Landon, and Ethan all looked up and greeted the two men, warmly. Of course Kenny knew them all well. Since their company used his construction company for several of their projects. They'd not only developed a solid business relationship, they'd become good friends.

"What makes you think we've been working?" Joshua Phoenix replied as the two men joined them.

"I know you all haven't left your beautiful wives on a Sunday night just to come sit in here and look at each other." Terry responded with a knowing grin.

"You're right." Ethan added. We figured since we had to work late on a Sunday, we may as well top off the evening with beer and basketball playoffs."

The atmosphere was loud and lively even though it was after nine on a Sunday night. A waitress approached the table to take the orders of the newcomers. Kenny wasn't much of a drinker, but tonight he felt like a tall cold beer. It had been a busy week and he'd been feeling uneasy for the past few days. He didn't know why because everything was going well. All the jobs were coming along great and the foreman he'd hired over a year ago was doing a terrific job.

Actually, Cliff was a close friend of his who took the job as a favor to Kenny and also because he loved the work. Cliff and Kenny also partnered in a security taskforce business. It was more than a security company, more like a mini version of the FBI and CIA rolled into one. They'd worked together for years doing independent work for the government.

Not only did he have to fire the last foreman, the man had been arrested for conspiracy to commit arson and conspiracy to commit intimidation. Unbeknownst to Kenny, Slate Jordan, his former foreman, was the nephew of a rival construction company, E.C. Timber, which lost the Enrich Corp bid to revitalize the old art district. He'd set it up to make it look like Cavanaugh Construction was trying to intimidate business owners to sell their business after renovations were done.

Ethan Powers nor Landon Phoenix ever believed Kenny or his company had anything to do with the intimidations. However, Kenny wasn't convinced that the duplicity stopped with E.C. Timber. He wasn't letting go of the idea that Slate Jordan's reign of terror had everything to do with his past. That's why he decided to bring in Cliff as foreman. He trusted him and Cliff was as knowledgeable in the construction business as Kenny. Together, they made a formidable team.

Kenny's thoughts briefly took him to another place—another time.

His past.

He could feel the darkness trying to creep in. Would that cloud forever hang over his head?

"Cavanaugh, you OK?" Landon asked.

Kenny realized he'd missed something because they were all looking up at him. "It's just been a long day."

Just then, the waitress arrived with beers for Kenny and Terry and another round for the other guys.

"Well, have a beer. There's nothing a beer and basketball can't cure." Landon raised his bottle, clinked it with Kenny's and both men took a long swig.

After a while, Kenny began to relax as he got into the game and conversations with the rest of the guys.

"Doesn't Symphony's officially open tomorrow?" Ethan asked no one in particular.

Kenny noticed Terry stiffen a bit. He didn't care what his friend said about being over Symphony, Kenny knew that it still bothered Terry to see her with her new husband. Terry's eyes never left the TV screen, but Kenny was sure he'd heard the question.

Kenny had to stop himself from blurting out, "Yes!" He knew Symphony's was opening in the morning. He also knew that Ricco worked until all hours of the night getting ready for the grand opening and was pretty sure she was there right now, trying to make sure everything was perfect.

He'd driven through the neighborhood often at night, telling himself it was because he was proud of the work he and his team had done, but his eyes always found the window above the bakery, to check to see if the light was on. It was where they'd built the office.

Joshua offered the answer. "Yes, it opens tomorrow. Actually they were all supposed to be here by now…" before he could finish his statement, Terry interrupted.

"You mean Symphony isn't here yet?"

All eyes turned to him. Kenny wanted to chuckle, but he knew the whole *Symphony situation* was eating his friend alive.

"As I was saying,"—Joshua gave Terry a look—"Cadence had a party they didn't want her to miss yesterday, and there is a bad storm down that way today, and it delayed their flight a few times. The last I heard from Alex, they may not even make it here for the opening."

Terry looked incredulous. "She's missing her own grand opening?"

"Well, Terry, marriage and motherhood tends to change your priorities." Ethan added. "I know for me, it did. I used to think that nothing was more important than my work, but after marrying Sophia, my perspective changed and after Bridgett, it changed even more—for both of us. She's no longer at the dance studio before dawn or until late at night, and I try to end my work day at five like most humans."

"Thanks for that little life lesson." Terry stated, each word short and clipped with annoyance.

"I didn't mean to sound condescending. I just know that sometimes it's difficult for others to understand."

Kenny knew that Ethan and his wife had an adopted daughter. Ethan made it his business to be at all of her recitals and programs at school.

"I get it." Terry snapped.

"We thought you were all good with Symphony and Kyle being together?" It was Joshua who spoke.

"Damn Josh, the man lost the love of his life to another dude. That's always going to sting just a little." Landon said to his brother. "Especially when that dude and the woman are around all the time."

"I'm right here. Stop talking about me like I'm not sitting at the damn table. Plus, you all know I'm seeing Ava."

"Yeah, and how's that going?"

Kenny wasn't sure which of the cousins asked the question nor did he hear an answer, he was still thinking about Ricco being at the shop getting ready for the grand opening.

The waitress walked up to check on them and she'd just walked away when Ethan's phone rang. Kenny watched the man groan and hesitate just a moment, before answering the call. Before Kenny could wonder if it was Ethan's wife calling, Kenny's phone rang as well. He frowned, wondering what Cliff wanted at this time of night.

"This better be good, Cliff." Kenny snapped into the phone. Kenny's eyes widened at the same time as Ethan quickly stood. He knew instantly that they were getting the same news.

A Fire.

Another one.

Kenny stood quickly as well. The other men looked at Ethan and Kenny. "What?" They all asked, standing too.

"There's been a fire. From the information I got from Samuel, it sounds like it may be Symphony's." Ethan said, hurriedly as he tossed money on the table.

"Damn!" Terry exclaimed.

Kenny's head snapped around to Ethan, he'd been pulling money from his own wallet for the beer he'd ordered. Cliff had not mentioned which of the buildings was on fire. "Was anyone there?" He asked.

"Don't know yet." Ethan replied.

Most people were so engrossed in the game playing on the TVs surrounding the bar, that it wasn't much noticed that the five men rushed from the place.

Kenny jumped in his pick-up truck and sped away, not giving a damn about the structure he'd worked tirelessly on for months and months. His sole focus was on the woman who may or may not be in that structure.

There was an alley that ran behind Symphony's. Symphony had requested the specific location, because of all the deliveries she received weekly. Kenny counted the exits in his head. *Front door, back door, window upstairs where he'd created an office, and of course there was a fire escape from the office.* Surely if she was there, it would have been easy for her to get out of the building. And because of the nature of the business it was equipped with special systems to extinguish fires.

The entire street was blocked off. Fire trucks, police vehicles and ambulances cluttered the area. Kenny hoped the latter was just a precautionary measure. Police officers weren't letting anyone through the barricades, they didn't care who he was and what he'd built. The Phoenixes fared no differently.

It was difficult to see around all the vehicles and people, but the smoke seemed to be coming from the back of Symphony's. All five men stood helplessly as smoke poured from the front of the bakery when the firefighters broke through the door.

Kenny couldn't breathe.

Vaguely, from his peripheral, he saw Joshua break away from their group. Kenny's eyes never left the front of the bakery.

Suddenly there was a bunch of shouting and gesturing. It sounded like he heard someone yelling, "We found one! We found one!"

One what?

A person?

Was it Naricco?

Kenny's throat constricted as Naricco's beautiful porcelain face, and straight jet-black hair filled his mind. He moved away from the men he'd arrived with and the police officer who stood next to the barricade keeping people away.

Several store owners that he knew from working with them, pressed closely, terror and panic claiming their features. The barricades stretched across the street to the opposite sidewalk. He noticed the officer on that end was called over near the fire trucks. Kenny slipped through the barricade, unnoticed, the smoke making it more difficult to breathe as he got closer to the building. He walked through the groups of first responders with such confidence and ease that no one questioned his presence.

"Is there someone in the building?" Kenny urgently addressed a young paramedic. Before he could answer, there was shouting near the entrance of the bakery.

"We need a stretcher over here!"

Kenny turned and before his mind could process the unconscious body in the arms of the fireman, his feet didn't hesitate. He pushed through the first responders, none of which had an opportunity to question who he was or where he'd come from. When he confirmed it was indeed Ricco lying lifeless in the arms of the soot covered fireman, he wanted to snatch her from the man and run away to some place safe, but knew he couldn't.

Kenny didn't have time to wonder why he felt such possessiveness for a woman he knew he couldn't possibly have. He'd spent time with her the night they met and for lunch the next day, because he couldn't help himself, but even with such a small amount of time with her, he knew her.

Kenny knew Naricco Maki.

Her eyes couldn't hide the pain she tried so desperately to forget. They also couldn't hide the trust she wanted to put in him. He'd been attracted to her from the moment they'd met and hoped they both could take advantage of her short visit to Boston. She'd flirted with him easily that night and he'd no problem with the idea of joining her in her hotel room, but there was something she'd said that made him really look at her.

They'd been talking about gentrification and her entire demeanor changed when Terry mentioned something about people being forced to the streets. "It's never simple to be forced to the streets." She'd stated, and had to immediately leave the table. He knew then that she was different. She was not a "casual fling" type of woman. She was a "hold on to forever" type of woman, the type he could not have.

Here she was.

The woman he wanted but could not have.

Unconscious of his reaction, he reached to stroke her face and was jerked away by someone he couldn't see.

"Sir, you need to clear the area!" It was a fireman.

Before Kenny could do anything stupid like punch the guy in the face, he found Terry was at his other side dragging him away. "Let them take care of her, man. They need to do their job." Kenny looked up at him and back at Ricco. They were giving her oxygen and placing her into the ambulance. He watched until they closed the doors and sped away with sirens blaring.

Winter Lightning

They changed planes in New York for their flight to Boston and finally landed at 3:27 AM. "We still have time to get to the shop." Symphony said to her husband. "I'll just throw some water on my face and change in the office." They both looked travel-weary and unkempt.

"Well, at least Cadence looks better than us." Kyle Dean looked down at his daughter in the stroller sound asleep. It was one of the many great things about her; once she was asleep, nothing could wake her. They were in baggage claim waiting for the carousel to begin turning. "Want to rent a car so we won't have to wake Alex and Josh at this hour?"

Symphony yawned and stretched. When she looked up she saw Alex and Joshua walking towards them. After handshakes and hugs, Symphony asked, "How did you know we were here?"

As Alex stooped to get a look at her Goddaughter in the stroller, she said, "I got an alert on my phone when your plane took off from Jacksonville. It told us when you would land, so here we are."

There was something peculiar in her friend's tone, Symphony thought, then dismissed the idea because of the lateness of the hour. Or was it early?

The carousel started to turn and the two men went to pull the luggage when the pieces came around. When they rolled the luggage to where their wives were standing, Symphony said, "Looks like we'll have to go straight to the shop, if we're going to make it for the opening. Sorry you guys had to get up so early to get us." Alex and Joshua exchanged a glance. "What?" Symphony asked, knowing immediately that something was wrong. "Alex?" She looked at her friend.

Alex began, "The shop…" Symphony watched Alex look up at Joshua.

"Isn't everything ready?" She asked.

Alex reached to place a hand on Symphony's arm.

"What is it?" Symphony asked again. Knowing for certain now that something was terribly wrong. Kyle placed his arm around her waist and pulled her close to him, instinctively knowing she would need his strength.

It was Joshua who spoke. "We tried to call, but you'd just gotten on the flight."

"What is it, Joshua?" She punctuated her words, demanding an answer. Symphony looked up at Kyle, his face just as intense as hers.

"There was a fire around nine o'clock at Symphony's." Symphony's hands flew to her mouth as her breath caught. Kyle held firmly to her as Joshua continued. "The fire itself didn't do much damage but the smoke and water from the hoses—" His voice trailed off.

"A *fire*?" she repeated disbelievingly. "*My* shop?"

Symphony looked around the baggage claim area, confused, not seeing anything. She was only conscious of her husband holding her and her words "a fire" and "my shop" rolling continuously in her head. How could there have been a fire? Ricco was a stickler for safety. Suddenly her head buzzed and her blood turned to ice. Symphony's eyes flew to Joshua's.

"Ricco!" She choked, her eyes stinging from the tears threatening there, because she also knew what kind of work ethic Ricco possessed. There was no way she would have been gone before nine on the night before the grand opening. Her eyes pleaded with Joshua, hoping for a favorable response. "Ricco?" The name coming out small and slightly hopeful.

"She'd fallen asleep at her desk."

Symphony swayed, but her husband was right there supporting her as he always was. Symphony didn't hear the rest of Joshua's words. Her head buzzed thinking about her friend.

This couldn't possibly be real.

Chapter 4

Another fire.

There was no way smoke should have reached the upstairs office without the alarms blaring. Kenny had more than a suspicion that this was another act of arson.

Why Symphony's?

Why now?

On his way to the hospital, he'd made a call to make arrangements for a team to keep an eye on Symphony's and the businesses adjacent to it. Cliff was already on it. He'd dispatched the men as soon as he heard about the fire. Symphony Dean definitely didn't need anyone trying to steal her expensive equipment and he didn't want anyone showing up trying to cover their tracks.

If they thought it was odd that he was at the hospital, no one said anything. Kenny knew he wouldn't be able to rest until he knew Naricco would be OK. She was an obsession that he couldn't seem to shake. Though he knew he had to try.

Ethan's wife, Sophia and Landon's wife Candice, joined their husbands in the wait for news on Ricco. Apparently both women had become good friends with her since she'd been running the Boston based Symphony's and were as worried as everyone else.

It was still odd to Kenny how all the Phoenixes treated Symphony like family. They hadn't even met Symphony until years after she and Terry broke up.

Kenny knew he was the odd man out. Yes, he was friends with all who were there, but he'd made it a point not to attend any functions where he knew Naricco would be. The wives probably thought he was only there because Kenny worked with their husbands.

He looked around the room. It didn't matter how much they tried to mask the cold, stale, space of an ER waiting room, it would never feel warm and welcoming. The modern décor would never cover the echoes of grief, panic, and despair.

Kenny remembered the early morning hour just like this one. He remembered the moment the doctor came out. That look. The blank look that told him she was gone.

"Hey man, you Ok?" Kenny was so lost in thought that he hadn't heard Terry. "Kenny, you OK, man?" Kenny looked at his friend. "What's on your mind, Ken?" Terry asked in a concerned whisper.

Kenny shook his mind free of the past. "It's just been a long night."

Terry didn't look convinced and Kenny could tell he was about to say something when the hospital doors opened and in rushed Joshua and Alex along with Symphony and Kyle Dean pushing their daughter in a stroller. Kenny also saw the shadow of regret cloud Terry's features, before it quickly faded away.

Kenny watched Landon, Ethan, and their wives stand to greet the Deans.

"Is there any news?" Symphony asked.

"Not yet." The reply came from both Candice and Sophia as they gathered her in a warm embrace.

"It's been hours and still nothing?"

Both women shook their heads.

After all the hugs were done, Kenny and Terry stood and approached the couple. Kenny worked with them both throughout the renovations process and had grown fond of Symphony and Kyle. Even though Terry had become one of his best friends, he found that he enjoyed hanging out with Kyle as well. He was a good guy who loved his wife and kid. They'd spent quite a bit of time together on and off the job site. Symphony was a stickler for details and didn't mind telling him when something was wrong or not up to her standards.

Symphony surprised him when she rushed into Kenny's arms grabbing him tightly. He had to quickly brace himself against the fierceness of her embrace. "I'm so sorry all your hard work is ruined." She said sincerely.

Was she kidding? Her shop was most likely severely damaged and she was worried about him.

"No, Symphony, I'm sorry you have to endure any of this. Don't worry about your shop. My guys will have it ready again in no time."

"All I care about right now is Ricco."

"Me too," he whispered. For the moment, not denying how much she meant to him. Symphony squeezed him tightly again, before letting him go. He reached for Kyle's hand and did the shake half embrace thing like men do.

Kenny pretended not to notice the awkward exchange between Symphony and Kyle with Terry. He wasn't so sure if he could be so civil to the man who stole his girl. Symphony gave Terry a stiff hug.

"Terry." Kyle said and nodded while extending his hand.

"Kyle." Terry replied before turning to Symphony. "I'm so sorry about your shop Symphony and I just know Ricco will be OK."

"How can you be so sure, Terry?"

Before he could answer the woosh of the ER doors captured everyone's attention. It was a firefighter. He walked up to the registration desk and handed over a leather purse. He wasn't wearing the heavy jacket he'd worn at the scene, but still wore his uniform pants and blue T-shirt. He still reeked of smoke. Kenny also noticed a couple of women on the other side of the waiting room, raising an interested brow at the man.

"I believe this belonged to the woman in the bakery. How is she?" He said. It was then that Kenny figured it was the firefighter who'd carried Ricco out of the building.

"There's still no word, sir."

Symphony rushed over to him. "I'm Symphony Dean. Do you know what happened? What started the fire?"

"No, ma'am. There's another team investigating how the fire started. When we were making sure there were no live embers, I came across this purse and thought I'd bring it here in case there was emergency contact info in there, plus I figured she'd need it. I wasn't sure if a spouse or boyfriend needed to be contacted. I also wanted to make sure she was OK." He looked around the room like he expected to see a man step forward. Turning back to Symphony, "I'm John, by the way."

Kenny squinted his eyes at the man.

Symphony placed a hand on his arm. "Thank you for getting her out of there."

"What's her name?" He asked.

"Naricco Maki." She paused and smiled, "Everyone calls her Ricco."

Kenny watched the nurse pull a phone out of Ricco's purse.

"Sometimes you can find health and emergency information from a person's phone."

"How can you get in her phone?" John asked.

"If they have it set up, you can see the information without needing a passcode." She punched a few buttons. "Oh good! Here it is. Her emergency person is Symphony James."

"That's me!" Symphony exclaimed. "I mean, it's my maiden name, but I'm Symphony James. Is there more information you need? Does this mean I get to speak to the doctor about Ricco?"

"Looks like we have all the information we need. I'll have them update her chart with what's listed here. Hopefully the doctor will be out soon to speak to you all."

Kenny noticed that the fireman didn't leave and didn't look like he was in any hurry to do so. He couldn't help but wonder why the man had such a personal interest in Ricco.

46

Everyone settled down again. Kenny heard the fireman say that he wanted to make sure Ricco was OK.

"Do you normally do this?" Kyle looked pointedly at John. "Follow up with people you save, I mean."

Kenny knew he liked Kyle. He was about to ask the man the same question. Apparently, it was a question all of the men had on their minds, because they all gave John their full attention waiting for his answer.

John looked around at all of them. He had to notice their unfriendly and suspicious looks on their faces. "Actually, I don't. There was just something about her that made me want to make sure she was alright. And when I found her purse, it was like a sign that I needed to see her again and check on her."

His answer seemed to satisfy everyone but Kenny and Kyle. Kyle glanced up at Kenny and they exchanged a speaking look. Kenny knew that Kyle didn't really buy that story just like he didn't. Kenny pulled out his cell phone and sent a text to Cliff.

Alex yawned and checked her watch. Symphony spoke to the group. "You guys don't have to hang around here, we'll let you know if there's news on Ricco."

No one seemed to want to go, but Alex finally said, "Let us take Cadence home with us. We'll leave my car for you guys. I met Joshua here before we picked you up from the airport."

"Ethan and I want to go check the site and find out if they have any idea how the fire started." Landon said, standing. "I'll meet you at home later this morning, sweetheart." He said to his wife, Candice.

Symphony looked at the fireman. "I know you've had a long night. If you leave me your number, I promise to call you as soon as I have news on Ricco." He looked unsure at first then nodded. Symphony punched his number into her phone as Kenny was committing it to memory, she thanked him again for saving her friend, for going out of his way to bring the purse, and checking on her. "Let me help you move Cadence's stuff to Joshua's SUV." She said to Alex.

Kenny sent another text to Cliff with the phone number.

Terry indicated that he wanted to go check the site as well and Kenny was torn between going and staying. Kenny watched Kyle watch John leave. When the man got well into the parking lot, Kyle looked at Kenny. Everyone had left the ER, but Kyle and Kenny. Cadence was still asleep in the stroller next to her father.

"What do you think of that guy?" Kyle asked him.

"My gut tells me he's bad news."

"Same."

"Just so you know, I had a team keep an eye on the property overnight. I didn't want anyone running off with any of your equipment."

Kenny realized that Kyle didn't question the word, "team" and had the distinct impression that Kyle knew exactly what kind of team he had in place.

"Are you in love with her?" Kyle's face was serious, but Kenny also detected a hint of hope there. "Never mind. You don't have to answer."

Kenny studied Kyle for a long moment. "I hardly know her."

"Irrelevant. I fell in love with Symphony before I even knew her name."

"Mrs. Dean?"

Both men turned towards a woman in a lab coat. "I'm Doctor Harley, is Mrs. Dean still here?"

Alex and Symphony returned to the waiting room at that moment. "Here I am! How is she!"

"Let's have a seat."

Kenny didn't like the sound of that. He looked around the waiting area, they were the only ones in there. Symphony sat next to her husband and Alex sat beside Kenny. The doctor sat next to Symphony.

"How is she?" Symphony's words were hesitant.

"Well, she inhaled a lot of smoke. She was unresponsive when the paramedics arrived, but we managed to bring her back."

Something inside of Kenny shattered. He was sure the others could hear the pieces rattling around inside of him.

"Bring her back?" Alex spoke the words that no one else could manage to say.

"Yes. She had no pulse."

"Oh my God." Symphony grabbed her husband's hand. Cadence began to whine. Alex happily picked her up and rocked her.

"Ms. Maki is in critical condition. We did a bronchoscopy to check the damage of her airways."

"Bronchoscopy?" Symphony questioned.

"Yes, we inserted a small scope in her airways. There was severe damage. Her right lung is collapsed and because of the damage in her airways, she had to be intubated."

"Oh my God." She said again. "When can we see her?"

"Currently, she's heavily sedated. We don't want her disturbed for a while."

"I can't see her?"

"Not for a while. We are monitoring her very closely. We need to keep her as calm as possible. She's in ICU. We're hoping by late afternoon she will be more stable for visitors. We will give you a call if anything changes."

Kenny knew that what she really meant was if it looked like they were losing her, they would call. The doctor left them and the weight of her words held them immobile for several moments.

How did this happen?

And even more important, was it arson?

Enough.

He was tired of running from his past and wondering if anything that went wrong was a planned attack on him.

It ended now.

He ended it now.

Chapter 5

"Seriously?" The word came out scratchy and jagged. It was still so difficult to speak, but she was excited.

"Yep. The doctor says you can leave this morning."

"Finally!"

Just then, Dr. Harley walked in. "Well, Naricco," she lifted her arms, gesturing around the room. "Are you ready to leave these grand accommodations?"

Ricco sat curled up in the recliner next to the hospital bed. She took a deep breath and said slowly, "As much as I've enjoyed all of you and appreciate the care I've received," she included Nurse Natalie in her smile and took another few breaths, "I'm ready to sleep in my own bed." She breathed heavily, still having a difficult time catching her breath, even a week after the fire.

"Your lungs look good and you'll be able to talk without the hoarseness or difficulty in another few days. However, it may take a few weeks for you to be able to move around like you're used to without the shortness of breath." The doctor gave Ricco a pointed look. "You will have to promise me to rest, rest, rest."

"When will I be able to go back to work?" Ricco knew the shop was almost ready to open…again.

Dr. Harley frowned. "I'm sorry but I want you home and resting for at least three to four weeks, but very light duty at work for a couple weeks after that."

"Three weeks!" Ricco grabbed her throat. "Ouch. That hurt." Her words were more of a whisper than before. Symphony had already assured her that it didn't matter how long it took for her to recover, she would still pay her as normal. Ricco definitely had a problem with getting paid without working, but there seemed to be nothing she could do about it. She was truly thankful that Symphony and Kyle were so generous.

"Yes, three to *four* weeks. And rest includes resting your voice as well. You must give yourself time to heal." Dr. Harley's face turned very serious. "By all rights you should be dead, Naricco Maki." Ricco flinched inwardly. Dr. Harley sat on the bed next to Ricco's chair. "By the grace of God, you are still with us." She punctuated her last words. "Give. Your. Body. Time. To. Heal." Dutifully chastised, Ricco nodded her head.

The doctor continued. "I'm not saying you're confined to your home. You may take short walks, even do a little shopping," she gave her a smile and a wink, "you can even go on a short dinner date. I've talked to Mrs. Dean. I know how hard you work. So no work...yes, to a date."

Ricco rolled her eyes. "There is no one to go on a 'short dinner date' with."

"You mean to tell me that during all these months you've been in Boston, you've not met anyone you wanted to date?"

Kenny immediately came to mind.

Why couldn't she forget about him like he'd so casually forgotten about and dismissed her. She looked up at Dr. Harley. Her throat was still on fire from the little talking she'd done already. She simply shook her head, "No."

No, there was no one to date.

All of her staff at Symphony's had come to the hospital to visit, but she was not friends with any of them, at least not yet. At the moment they were her employees and she the boss. Each of them had come once and brought flowers and other gifts. They all got along well, but Ricco hadn't had time to develop any relationships with the people she worked with. They were too busy trying to get Symphony's opened in time for the grand opening date.

Natalie, the day nurse, spoke up, "Don't be so certain there won't be one in the future. John hasn't been coming around her for nothing. And I've seen some of the cute guys you work with."

John. The firefighter.

He was definitely good looking and he *had* been to visit her nearly every day since she'd been out of ICU. They hadn't had much conversation due to her inability to speak without much pain, but he was very sweet. Bringing her little trinkets from his firehouse. She was actually wearing a T-shirt from the station.

"Do you have someone you want us to call to pick you up?"

"If you need a ride, I can bring you home." They all turned to the male's voice coming from the doorway.

It was John.

Ricco smiled as he walked into the room. "Am I interrupting anything?"

"Actually, we're about to send Ms. Maki home."

He looked at Ricco. "I can bring you home. You won't have to disturb anyone to come get you. I'm already here."

Ricco frowned and shook her head to object. He handed her a little figurine of a fireman carrying a woman in his arms. "I was bringing this to you. Something for you to remember me."

"How could I possibly forget my real-life personal hero?" She whispered.

"As your real-life personal hero, it is only my duty to rescue you from this hospital."

"But I have all this stuff." She waved at all the flowers and gifts she'd received from her friends who were starting to feel more like family. Symphony, her husband, and the entire Phoenix clan had become a part of her life and they made her feel like she was a part of theirs.

"No problem, I'm in my SUV, today. I'm not taking 'no' for an answer." He turned to Dr. Harley. "How long before I can whisk her out of here?"

"I have all the paperwork, right here. Natalie will help you with it, Ricco, and then you are free to go. I'll see you in six weeks to hopefully give you your release to go back to work." She turned to John. "As her personal real-life hero, your job is to make sure she takes it easy. Rest is very important."

Traitor! Ricco thought.

John looked down at her and smiled, "Will do, doc."

If she had to have a personal hero, John fit the bill. He was the iconic tall, dark, and handsome. And unless she was mistaken, it appeared that he may have a hint of Asian in his largely European features. She was pretty sure at least one of his grandparents was Chinese. The man was simply gorgeous. She had to admit, she wanted to get to know him.

"Hello." She whispered, trying not to sound like a dying woman. "Don't I have a say in anything?" She tried to take slow steady breaths so she wouldn't appear so weak.

"Sure you do." Dr. Harley replied to her. "Do you want John to take some of these things down now while you sign the paperwork and get dressed or wait until you're all ready to go down."

Ricco shook her head. She waved around the room and then whispered, "Now."

Natalie ran out to grab a cart for John to begin loading up her flowers and gifts. Thirty minutes later all the papers were signed and she was packed and ready to go.

Several of the nurses on the floor came in to say goodbye to Ricco. She'd become quite fond of all of them. Natalie entered with a wheelchair. The chariot that would carry her down to John's vehicle. Reluctantly, she was starting to feel a little giddy about her fireman. She could tell he really liked her. He'd visited every day. One day when she still couldn't talk, she'd typed out on her iPad, "Am I the first girl you've saved from a burning building?"

He replied, "No, you aren't, but you're the first that I couldn't stop thinking about."

With that, she'd looked at him, smiled, and typed, "OK."

So, now, here she was about to leave the hospital with the man who'd saved her life. She guessed that she couldn't be in better hands. She positioned herself to be able to stand and sit in the wheelchair.

"Hello, Naricco."

Everyone looked towards the doorway except Ricco. There was no one who said her name quite that way.

Why was he here?

When she hadn't responded, John looked down at her stuck between sitting and standing. She ignored that, but she couldn't ignore the way the nurses were still staring open-mouthed at him. Before she knew it, Kenny had placed a vase of flowers on the bedside tray and was at her side. How the hell had he gotten next to her so quickly. He was supporting her arm so she could stand. She tried not to let everyone know how the heat of his touch burned her. She also didn't want to give away how shocked she was to see Kenny in her hospital room.

Why was he here?

Ricco allowed him to help her as to not give the nurses something to gossip about and did her best not to sit so heavily in the chair. She was still so weak and couldn't help how she had to depend on him for support. With a clenched jaw, she struggled to catch her breath.

"Hi." She took a few more breaths, "Kenny."

"I take it you're about to leave." He asked and after a few moments of just staring up at him, she nodded, because she didn't have the breath or the words to speak. Kenny looked at John, who wore a shadow of annoyance.

"John." Kenny stated flatly. "I didn't think I'd see you again."

Ricco raised a brow.

What in the hell was going on here?

Ricco looked from one man to the other. She wanted to ask how they knew each other but decided to save the question for later, because the few nurses who were still in her hospital room watched the exchange with way too much interest.

"Is Symphony or someone coming to collect you?" Kenny asked in a tone that suggested more familiarity than he had a right to.

"I'm bringing her home." It was John who spoke up then, answering Kenny's question as if he was staking his own claim on her.

For a moment she saw something flash across Kenny's features, but wasn't sure what and it was gone so quickly she thought she may have imagined it. Surely it was her imagination, because what she thought she saw was envy and suspicion.

She watched Kenny study the man for several uncomfortable moments before turning back to her. "Well, I just wanted to stop by and see how you were doing." He gestured to the flowers. "I brought these for you."

She nodded in appreciation at the exotic bouquet, still stunned to see him there. She wondered again, *why* he was there. He looked like he wanted to say more, but didn't.

Ricco was so confused. The last time she'd talked to Kenny he'd told her that it would be better if they didn't see or talk to each other anymore. And that was after a beautiful day together. The day she was supposed to leave Boston, but decided to spend more time with him. She'd felt so completely hurt and mortified. She'd been too embarrassed to tell Symphony how he'd treated her.

Winter Lightning

Now here he was showing up at her hospital door with flowers like they were the best of friends. Or better yet, like he gave a damn about her. The more she thought about it, the more pissed off she became.

She knew immediately when he realized what she was thinking. The bastard had the nerve to throw her that cocky smile of his and a wink.

He actually winked at her.

The nurses, not giving a care in the world about their little tete-ta-tete, were interested in the man standing in front of them. Where John was the classic tall, dark, and handsome, with a strong jawline and exotic dark eyes, Kenny, on the other hand, was mysteriously jaw-droppingly gorgeous. His eyes were like lightning and seemed to see all your sins. The silver streaks in his hair made his eyes even more vivid. Both men looked as if they saw the inside of a gym frequently, but there was something about Kenny Cavanaugh's presence that was so commanding and oh so good to look at. He wore his clothes like they were tailored just for him and he always walked like he knew where he was going.

Upset with herself, this time, for so quickly forgetting how pissed she was with him. This man turned her completely upside down.

"Are you ok, Naricco?"

It took her a beat or two, but she finally remembered where she was and that she had an audience.

"Thank you for coming by," she breathed through teeth she tried not to grit. He needed to get the hell out of there.

"Take care of yourself." He said to her and turned to leave. "John." He nodded at the man standing at her side.

"Cavanaugh." John returned, just as tersely.

Ricco inhaled as deep a breath as she could and let it out slowly.

What was that all about?

Chapter 6

Cavanaugh!

That bastard had called him Cavanaugh. At no point had he given his name. Even if he'd heard one of the others call him Kenny, he knew for certain that his last name had not been spoken that morning he met the fireman.

Kenny tried to calm down. He didn't want to jump to conclusions. At some point if John had come up to the hospital, someone could have said his name, but there was something not on the up and up with John Y. Parker. Kenny definitely knew his name and was going to find out as much as he could about *John*. What worried Kenny was that the fireman was using his career and the fact that he saved her life, to foster trust and get closer to Ricco. Hell, she was wearing a T-shirt from his fire station! Kenny needed to figure out why the man was still hanging around.

Kenny had kept Ricco at bay to keep her safe, but now he realized the only way to keep her safe, may be to get closer to her—not an easy task based on their previous dealings.

He could see it in the set of her face that she was pissed he'd shown up at the hospital.

63

In the hospital parking lot he pulled out his phone. "Yeah, it's me. She's being checked out today… You know what to do… Parker is bringing her home…That's what I thought too. No, I didn't…I don't think that would have gone over well…Enough with the questions. Just have the guys get into position and we may want to put a tail on Parker to see where he goes when he leaves Ricco's place."

Kenny clicked off the phone.

Damn.

Kenny pulled up at Cliques for his meeting with Landon, Ethan, and Kyle. He wasn't sure what this meeting was all about, but had a pretty good idea. He was also still thinking about his encounter with Ricco at the hospital. He'd almost laughed at the look on her face when she saw him.

The sport's bar was crowded as usual. It was just eleven o'clock, but there was already a wait for tables. In the evenings, the club upstairs was also always packed. Kenny spotted the guys and joined them at the table.

"But I thought the fire chief said it was electrical?" Kyle asked.

"Yes that was the report that was filed." Ethan replied.

"But you don't believe that?"

"No." Ethan looked at Kenny.

Kenny's eyes went to Kyle. "Jacob Lewis is the best electrician in New England. Kenny stated as he took a seat, immediately joining the conversation.

"He's the one that did the wiring?"

"Yes, and the entire structure was rewired. Lewis inspected the wires after the fire and found nothing that would have caused a fire." Kenny paused. "In fact, none of the wires were even charred."

Kyle sat up. "Are you saying that someone deliberately set that fire?" Before anyone could answer, Kyle frowned and continued. "That means the fire chief knowingly lied in his report." It was a statement. Kyle looked around the table at all the faces staring back at him. He sat back in the chair. Kenny could only imagine what the man was thinking--the safety of his wife being paramount.

"We're not so sure. It could be that the chief just took the word of other firefighters doing the inspections and didn't check for himself."

"Ricco nearly died." That statement caused Kenny's chest to tighten. He knew well how close to death she'd come. "Does any of this have anything to do with the fire over a year ago?" Kyle asked.

Ethan looked at Kenny before answering Kyle. "We don't know."

"Wait…Is Symphony in any danger?" Kyle asked. The question asked more urgently than the rest.

"We don't think so." Landon finally spoke.

"Forgive me if I don't feel much comfort from, 'we don't think so.'"

Kenny knew what the man was thinking. Symphony's was due to open in another few days and Symphony had been working side by side with Kenny's guys, day and night.

"Because I thought of the same thing, Kyle, I've hired a security company to keep an eye on the area. Symphony's especially." No one knew that he was part owner in that security company, nor did he want to tell them that he was quite confident that Symphony was safe. It was Ricco he was most worried about.

The night he'd met her, he'd called in a favor to a guy he knew in the Bureau to get Ricco's cell number. In hindsight it now seemed to have been a mistake. It could be a coincidence, but Kenny didn't want to rule out that someone may have connected him to Ricco and is using her as some sort of warped revenge.

"Did any of you know that Ricco was being checked out of the hospital today?"

Kyle looked at Kenny, confused. "What do you mean? Ricco didn't mention anything when she talked to Symphony this morning. We're supposed to go visit her after I leave you guys."

"I stopped by to see her before I came to Cliques." Kenny ignored the curious looks from Ethan and Landon. "When I got there all the nurses were telling her goodbye and that firefighter was there." Kenny knew they all knew who he meant. "He was bringing her home."

Kyle's eyes narrowed. "I don't trust that guy."

"Neither do I," Kenny agreed.

"What's the deal with the firefighter?" Landon asked. "What's his name? John?"

"Yeah, that's him." Kyle said, his tone filled with annoyance. "How many firefighters show up at the hospital to check on someone they pulled out of the fire? I mean, the guy even admitted that it was unusual for him."

"Maybe he's just attracted to Ricco. I mean she is a beautiful woman."

Kenny tried not to level a piercing look at Ethan and did his best to keep his tone casual. "How did he happen to be bringing her home? She has friends here."

"How is it that you happened to be at the hospital?" Landon asked. "I didn't even know you knew Ricco. I also couldn't help but notice how you broke through the barricade when she was brought out of Symphony's that night."

He kept his tone casual enough. "I was concerned. I felt responsible since my company had done the work. I just wanted to make sure she would be OK." His excuse sounded plausible, but Kenny knew they weren't buying what he was saying. However, they had the decency to pretend they were.

They finished their lunches and afterwards, went their separate ways. Kyle said he would stop by the shop to get Symphony so they could go check on Ricco. Kenny thought about what type of plan he needed to put into place to gain Ricco's trust again and get closer to her.

Chapter 7

It was nice for him to give her a ride home and help her with all the gifts she'd gathered over the past week, but he seemed to want to visit. She was not up for visiting. Especially not with someone new. And especially right out of the hospital. She had to admit that she did like John, but she *had* just gotten out of the hospital and every single thing made her exhausted.

John was a really nice guy and she was super appreciative of him saving her life, but she didn't have any qualms about sending him away when he became clingy. He was, after all, a virtual stranger. He wanted to help her put everything away, but she stopped him in her foyer, thanked him for the ride, and sent him away. She did, however, have to agree to go to a Firemen's ball with him to get him out of her apartment. He was very persistent and she was completely exhausted. She'd given him her number when he asked if he could have it to check on her in the meantime. She figured she'd call and cancel about the ball, feigning exhaustion or something.

Symphony and Kyle arrived a while after he left and helped her get settled. Their company, she didn't mind. They were, after all, the only family she had.

She'd showered, donned some fresh pajamas, and settled herself on the sofa before they agreed to leave her alone. She loved them and preferred their company over John's but she really just wanted to finally be left alone. For the past two weeks she'd been poked, prodded, and disturbed constantly. Now, she could finally have a chance to marvel in the fact that she was home.

Ricco was glad she didn't remember anything about the fire. She didn't need anything else to plague her thoughts. All she remembered was placing her head on her desk and waking a day later with a tube down her throat—unable to speak. The following day was a blur because she'd been heavily sedated.

A thought just occurred to her. Did Kenny meet John at the hospital? Had he come after she'd been brought in? Is that how he knew his name? John told her that he'd been at the hospital after she was brought in. He mentioned that several people were there, concerned. However, he had not mentioned who.

If Kenny had shown up in the emergency room or any other time at the hospital, why had he done it? He'd made it crystal clear, over a year ago, that there could be nothing between them and it was best that they didn't see each other again or communicate via phone.

He'd been the balm she needed that night—comforting, perfect, and passionate. And even the next day, they'd shared what she thought, a wonderful time at lunch. The closer they'd gotten to the airport, the more distant he became. By the time they'd arrived, she may as well have been in a cab. She'd been so taken aback by his behavior, she didn't know what to say when he shook her hand and gave her a chaste kiss on the cheek after helping her place her luggage on the curb.

What happened? What happened to the warm compassionate guy she'd known only hours before? And to top it off, when she went through security she received a text from Kenny telling her that it probably wasn't a good idea if they saw each other again. He wished her a pleasant flight and told her to take care. Too stunned to react, she simply put her phone away and tried to put him out of her thoughts.

Ricco's eyes fell on the flowers in the pretty green vase.

Cherry blossoms!

Where in the world did he find cherry blossoms? She'd loved seeing them in full bloom when she'd visited her grandmother in her little village of Yoshino in Japan.

Ricco's doorbell rang and she groaned out loud. Who in the hell was visiting her here? The only people who'd come to her condo before, were Kyle and Symphony. And who else knew she was even out of the hospital? Plus, no one else ever came to visit her.

Well, she figured it wouldn't be too difficult to find out she'd been released, but she still didn't know of anyone who would come to her home. She eased herself up and made her way to the front door. If it was John, she would truly be annoyed and tell him so. Ricco looked through the peephole and her breath caught. She couldn't tell if she was having difficulty breathing because of who it was or if it was her lungs still struggling to fill with air.

Kenny Cavanaugh!

How the hell did he even know where she lived?

The only thing she knew for certain was there were always so many questions surrounding this man and his actions. And for the life of her, she wanted answers to her questions. She swung the door open wide. Ricco just stared at him.

Winter Lightning

It didn't take long to realize that staring at him was a huge mistake. Oh my goodness, those eyes of his. They were so magnetic, electrifying—they crackled and sparked. She could swear little embers burned her wherever his eyes touched her and right now he held her gaze with so much intensity, her eyes literally burned.

She rolled her eyes just to break the contact.

"Twice in one day. I feel like I won the lottery." She stood there in her fleece pajama bottoms and purple camisole looking up at him, hating that her words were coming out in a gravely whisper.

He had the nerve to grin.

Sexy bastard.

Standing there in her bare feet made him a good foot taller than she.

"Are you familiar with Shirley Jackson?"

He frowned, "No."

"She's an author. She wrote a short story called, 'The Lottery.' It's one of the stories I had to read in an American literature class when I came to university." Ricco clinched her teeth and sighed. "I mean when I came here to go to college." She'd spent so much time trying to fit in, that correcting colloquial phrases from home, was still a habit.

"Seeing you twice in one day, makes me feel like I won the lottery, like the woman in that story. His eyes narrowed. She turned and walked away, leaving the door open, knowing he would follow. "Surely you must have a *grand* reason for being here." She threw her hands up and wide, sarcasm dripping from every word. The effort cost her precious energy and breath. She just needed to lie down.

"I do."

Ricco resumed her position, curled up on the sofa with the blanket up to her neck. "Are you going to tell me or is it a secret?" He sat in a chair next to the sofa, near her head.

"I wanted to see you." The sincerity of his words was so unexpected that she was completely stuck. She couldn't speak, blink, or think beyond his statement. "Besides earlier today, the last time I'd lain eyes on you, you were unconscious in another man's arms." His words were thick with emotion—that, too, surprised her.

She. Would. Not. React. To. This!

She. Just. Would. Not!

What in the entire hell was he talking about? Why was he saying these things to her? Why did he sound like he'd experienced some sort of emotional torment?

Ricco was tossed between anger and enchantment. Her throat tightened and it had nothing to do with her injuries.

She stared dry-eyed at Kenny.

He crossed his legs and peered at her like she was some sort of case study. Suddenly, she felt too small—too vulnerable. She eased herself into a sitting position and willed her lungs to cooperate.

"Are you for real?" She asked, incredulous.

"I am whatever you want me to be, Naricco."

Ricco's eyes widened, narrowed, and then glared at this man sitting in her living room. This man who had the gall to be witty, charming, and arrogant all at once. This man who'd once made her feel warm and safe. This man who'd made her *feel*.

She took a deep breath so her words would arrive as clear and as strong as she could muster.

"Get out."

She could tell he wanted to object, to say something, but had the very good sense to keep his mouth shut and do as she demanded.

Stoically, he stood and walked out.

She watched him turn the knob to lock the door before he closed it behind him.

Ricco needed a distraction. She picked up the phone to call Symphony. "I need a favor."

"Sure, what do you need?"

Ricco could hear chatter in the background. "I'm sorry, did I catch you at a bad time?"

"No, Alex and Sophia just stopped by to check on the progress at the shop and to ask me how you're doing. I'm going to put you on speaker. They've been wanting to talk to you." Ricco could hear Symphony talking away from the phone. "It's Ricco. She can't talk long, but I know you guys are worried about her."

"Hey, Ricco!" They both sang in unison.

"Hey ladies."

"Do you need anything? What can we do?" Alex and Sophia asked in turn.

"Well actually, I was calling Symphony, because I need a ball gown and don't think I have the strength to do any shopping right now."

There was a pause. "Ummm…that's not what we were expecting you to need, fresh out of the hospital." Symphony stated, with a bit of confused humor in her voice.

"Are you going to the firemen's ball with that sexy fireman? Ohhh caliente!" Sophia blurted in her rich Venezuelan accent.

The soft laugh was all Ricco could muster at the moment.

Winter Lightning

"You're going to a ball? Isn't it too soon for you to be going out?" Symphony asked, concerned. Ricco knew Symphony couldn't help being a mother hen, but the question irritated her.

"The doctor only limited me from work. She specifically encouraged me to go on a date." Silence. Ricco sighed. "I didn't mean to snap at you, Symphony. I'm just tired."

"Don't apologize. I'm sorry for sounding like an overbearing mom. You're smart enough to take care of yourself."

"Oh Ricco!" Sophia chimed in. "We just got racks of dresses from some designers in New York. Donations for an upcoming show at my performing arts school. I'm sure we'll be able to find something for you in there."

"Really?" Ricco whispered excitedly.

"Sure we can. How about we bring over some dresses for you to try on, in a few days after you've rested up a bit?"

"That sounds great."

They all said their goodbyes and Symphony promised to bring over some dinner in a few hours. Ricco was exhausted, but was beginning to get a little excited about the prospects of the ball and spending time with John.

*****

Well, that didn't go well at all.

Kenny knew it wasn't going to be easy, but he wasn't prepared to be sliced open by the look on her face. Every time he saw her, he just wanted to gather her into his arms and take all her pain away. It tore him up knowing that he was the one causing it.

Her feelings were hurt.

Her beautiful exotic ebony eyes told him that she felt hurt and betrayed. And he'd been the one to do it to her. He'd been the one to give her safety and comfort and then rip it away from her.

And what did she mean by that statement about winning the lottery. Pulling out his phone, he did a search for "The Lottery" by Shirley Jackson. The synopsis of the story didn't tell him much except the townspeople gathered for the annual lottery. He clicked a few more links and found out the person chosen for the lottery is stoned to death.

Damn.

That's how she felt? Like he'd stoned her to death?

"Well fuck." He whispered aloud.

Kenny placed the key in the ignition and turned it. There was a single click and a hum. Every hair on his body stood on end. He didn't remove the key nor did he open the car door. He didn't even bother to reach for his phone. It was too dangerous. He knew that one of his men would wonder why he hadn't moved. After about twenty-five minutes had passed, he saw Cliff coming down the sidewalk like he was window shopping. When he reached the shop across from his truck, he looked especially interested in the items displayed. Kenny could tell he was watching him in the reflection. Kenny was thankful there weren't more people on the streets.

Kenny signaled Cliff and the man immediately sprang into action. Cliff punched in a number on his cell phone and minutes later a tow truck appeared along with what looked like another roadside assistance car. The two men from the car and the two from the truck jumped out of their vehicles and began to carefully inspect Kenny's truck. It took them about thirty seconds to find a device programmed to cause the ignition to heat the gas tank enough to ignite an explosion. They weren't sure when someone rigged it in there, because they'd been watching Ricco's home since she'd arrived from the hospital. Just from looking, one of the guys guessed there was a computer chip that could be triggered remotely.

Triggered remotely.

He'd parked maybe ten yards from her door.

Ten yards.

That was way too close for comfort. Getting closer to her was proving to be far too dangerous right now. He needed to figure out who had a vendetta against him.

Chapter 8

"Well Naricco Maki, you do clean up well." Ricco said to the mirror. She looked over her shoulder, "What do you think?"

"Mighty fine, my friend, mighty fine." Symphony made the statement with such seriousness that both women fell into laughter. "Your fireman will have to extinguish *himself* when he sees you."

"He's not *my* fireman." Ricco told her flatly. She admitted that she was a little nervous and excited, but it didn't really have anything to do with John. He was handsome, but she hadn't really made any kind of connection with him. There was no spark—no caliente, as Sophia would say.

Symphony went back to her own place. They lived in the same building. Ricco lived in one of the smaller townhomes and Symphony had one of the larger ones in the building adjacent to hers.

Over the past week, John called her several times to check on her and to make sure she was still going to the ball. It was his first one as well so he didn't know what to expect either. She hadn't heard from Kenny since the day she put him out of her home. She told herself that she'd not agreed to go out with

John just to get over the effects of Kenny. John was a nice guy and she wanted to take this opportunity to get out and meet people and spend time with him.

Yes. That was it. It had nothing to do with Kenny Cavanaugh.

Kenny.

Why had his presence been so potent? His voice, his eyes, the way he held her, his kiss—

The doorbell rang, startling Ricco from her musings.

"Wow!" John replied when she opened the door. "You are adorable."

She tried her best to hold her smile in place, but being called adorable wasn't quite the compliment she was going for. Adorable was for little girls heading to the Daddy Daughter dance with their fathers. He, on the other hand, was very dashing in his dress uniform. "You look very nice, too." She said, and meant it.

"You ready?" He asked.

"Sure. Let me grab my bag." Ricco resisted the urge to roll her eyes and lock herself in her bedroom until she thought he was gone, but instead, she took a deep breath and decided to enjoy herself tonight. Her doctor and friends were right. Dating may be fun and would get her mind off of the fire and not working. She was nowhere near full strength, but to those who didn't know her, it just sounded as if she was soft spoken and quiet. She'd tried building her stamina by walking around her apartment and working her way up and down the steps. She was still using the downstairs bedroom, where she grabbed her purse off the end of the bed and wondered what her evening with John would bring.

Ricco slid into the passenger seat of the sleek silver sports car. It was a convertible and he had the top down. "You own two vehicles?" Not caring if the question was rude or not. The last time she'd ridden with him, he drove a nice SUV.

"Yes. Every now and then, I like to drive fast and look cool while I'm doing it."

He missed the tiny eye roll, because he was too busy checking out his own car.

"I like your car, but are we going to ride with the top down?"

Confusion clouded his face, which confused her.

"I thought women liked riding with the top down."

"Well, yeah, we do, but not when we're dressed for a formal evening and we've spent an undisclosed amount of time getting our hair just right." Why did she have to explain this to a grown man?

He looked up at her head as if thinking she couldn't have possibly spent much time on her hair.

"No worries." He said finally

Her hair was softly pulled back in a very intricate bun at the base of her neck. Sophia and Symphony had spent nearly two hours on it with Ricco's instructions. She thought it was pretty stunning and it irked her that he was so clueless about women that he would suggest riding with the top down.

He put the top up before heading towards the hotel where the ball was being held.

"Has work been busy lately? Rescuing damsels in distress?" She tried her best at small talk, but in actuality she hated idle chit chat.

"Not lately, thank goodness." He turned onto a busy street. Even she knew there was a more indirect way to get downtown that would avoid evening traffic and she wondered why he wasn't going that way. He seemed to be concentrating on where he was going. Everyone knew this street was horrible at this time of night. "Lately, our station has been replying to mostly wrecks and people collapsing in places." He saw all the red lights from the stopped vehicles in front of him and let out what sounded like a mumbled curse, but she didn't recognize what he said.

"This street is hit or miss. You never know what the traffic is going to be like." She offered. Have you lived in Boston long?"

"I thought I'd lived here long enough to know how to avoid the traffic."

He didn't answer her question and she didn't press. He was annoyed by the traffic and she was annoyed that he was annoyed by the traffic. In his profession he should be more familiar with traffic flare-ups. All of a sudden, his irritation faded and he sat up straighter.

"There seems to be thousands of red lights ahead of us. How many do you think there are?"

Immediately, all the red dots multiplied in her head and she knew exactly how many there were and nearly blurted it out, but didn't. People tended to look at her like she was some sort of science project when she knew the exact number of things. So she just said, "There's a bunch of them." John's jaw tightened and then quickly relaxed.

"Yeah. Sorry. I should have gone a different way."

Ricco didn't say anything. She chalked her uneasiness up to not being on the dating scene in a long time, plus she was irritated easier since the episode from the fire. "What can I expect tonight? I've never been to a ball." She tried to lighten the mood, change the vibe—something.

"The usual stuff...dinner and speeches, and then mingling and dancing. I guess. At least that's what a guy at work said. This is my first time too."

"Do you dance?"

"Yes, I love to dance."

She was surprised by that. Most men she knew didn't do much dancing. "I'm not sure how much dancing I'll be able to do. I get winded so easily, lately."

Ricco tried not to think of Kenny, heaven knows she didn't want thoughts of him to infuriate her, but there was absolutely no chemistry between her and John.

She sighed heavily. Maybe she wasn't trying hard enough. "So tell me a little about yourself, John." He had a blank look on his face. "What made you want to be a fireman?"

"My father was a fireman. I grew up in Wisconsin. I have two sisters and one brother. My mother's name is Meg."

Well, she'd asked, but she was expecting more of a narrative than a list of facts.

"What about you? Where did you grow up?"

Ricco had answered that question many times over the years. "I grew up in Florida. I just love being around the sunshine and beautiful beaches." She went on to tell him about hanging out with some of her college friends on the beaches instead of going to classes, but she still managed to do well in school. "Where did you go to college?" She asked him.

"Did you spend lots of time at Disneyland?"

"Disneyland is in California, we have Disney World in Florida." She noticed how he sidestepped her question, but didn't call him out on it.

They finally made it to the hotel. The line of cars with formally dressed people exiting them told her the evening would be well attended.

Chapter 9

His back was to the door, but he knew the moment she stepped into the ballroom. His date, Lynnette, was rambling on about her two cats that couldn't seem to get along no matter how much training she'd paid for.

It had taken her fifteen minutes to pet, coo, and coax them into their little cat cages. Lynnette called them little lounge rooms. The woman had literally shed a tear having to kennel them. Saying her sitter had canceled on her at the last minute. She'd contemplated canceling, but missing the ball would have been frowned upon by her chief.

That episode alone should have told Kenny this entire idea was not a sound one. He kept telling himself he was doing it to keep Ricco safe, but he knew deep down it was because he was jealous and the green-eyed monster was eating him alive.

The moment he'd overheard Symphony, Sophia, and Alex talking about dressing Ricco for the event, first he worried about her doing too much too soon, and then when he realized who'd she'd most likely been invited by, suspicion and plain old jealousy took over.

He'd met Lynnette at Cliques one evening. She'd flirted relentlessly and even though it had been ages since he'd had a woman in his bed, he had no desire for Lynnette—not in that way. It had taken her all of two minutes to start talking about her cats. Her saving grace that evening was finding out she was a firefighter.

He'd felt like a cad, but he had to get to that ball. So he called her up and invited her out. It took two miserable dates before she insisted they go to the fireman's ball together.

And here he was. Elbow deep in scotch, the beginning of headache from her incessant chatter, and a strong desire to throw the entire plan out the window.

What was his plan anyway?

"Kenny, did you hear what I said? Peek-a-boo ended up with a thorn stuck in his paw."

Kenny felt like he had a thorn stuck in his—

"Kenny!" She looked thoroughly disgusted that he didn't appear to be interested in her story.

"My apologies Lynnette. I thought I heard someone call my name." He turned then, not able to keep himself from doing so.

Struck dumb and immobile, Kenny could no longer see anyone except Ricco. It looked as if she was speaking to someone she'd just been introduced to.

She'd extended her hand and smiled politely to an older gentleman in a fireman's dress uniform.

Kenny did not and could not hear Lynnette saucily trying to get his attention. He only felt his heart slam into his ribs—shaking him to the core. He wasn't sure if it was the sight of her poured into a beautiful form-fitting emerald gown, his favorite color, or if it was the scotch buzzing around his brain, but he suddenly felt very unsteady on his feet.

"Kenny!" Lynnette harshly whispered as she yanked on his arm. "Am I boring you?"

He wanted to tell her the truth, but instead tried to dazzle her with his most charming smile. To his delight, she was left speechless. "I see an acquaintance of mine, I'd like to speak to. Do you mind?"

Still apparently reeling from his smile, she nodded and slipped her hand possessively in the crook of his arm. Kenny, feeling a bit buzzed and chastising himself for drinking so much scotch, made a B-line to Ricco. He tried not to be annoyed by the many interruptions on his quest. Lynnette and he were stopped many times by her co-workers, present and former, and even by people he'd done business with over the years. The ball was to honor the firemen, so it was heavily attended by city officials and Kenny was acquainted with many people there. He was, in his own right, an icon in his community, but he never really thought of himself that way. He saw himself as just a contractor.

When he looked up again, Ricco and the fireman had found their seats. He watched the man pull out her seat, place his hand way too low on her back—Kenny's buzz suddenly gone, he made his way to her—damn the interruptions. As providence had it, Lynnette announced that they were to sit at the same table.

"Oh look! My friend John is at our table. I want you to meet him."

"Have the two of you known each other long?" He asked her. If it was an odd question, she made no indication of it.

"He's only been in our unit a few months. I can't remember where he was before." She paused. "I wonder how he ended up with that oriental woman."

Kenny stiffened. Surely no one was still closed-minded enough to refer to anyone with slanted eyes as oriental. "A rug may be considered oriental, but not a person." He said, in a simmering soft tone, just barely able to contain his fury.

She waved him off and giggled. "You know what I mean."

Kenny had the impulse to snatch himself away from her body clinging to him and wanted to abandon this fool idea of spying on Ricco, just so this simpleminded woman would be nowhere near Ricco.

"John!" Lynnette shouted, causing a few heads to turn. "John!" John turned and gave her a huge smile, until his eyes landed on Kenny. His excitement of seeing his friend faltered for an instant when his eyes narrowed and darkened. John's expression quickly recovered. "Hi John. I'm so glad we're at the same table. I was afraid I'd be stuck talking to some of these old stuffy bitties."

A few women looked up at Lynnette who didn't seem to have a clue as to how rude and embarrassing she was. John, on the other hand, looked anything but excited to be at the table with her and Kenny. "This is Kenny, my—"

"Date." Kenny added quickly, before Lynnette got any ideas about them being a couple.

"Ah…Mr. Cavanaugh, I must say this is a complete surprise to see you. If it didn't sound so foolish, I'd say you were keeping tabs on our beautiful Ricco."

"Well it is no surprise to see you, John." He stressed the name as if it was an insult. "After all, it is a fireman's ball, however, I am indeed surprised to find you here with *our* beautiful Naricco."

"You know each other?" A frowning Lynnette asked the two men.

By this time, Ricco noticed the conversation going on above her. Kenny knew she'd been engaged in conversation with a woman seated next to her. He'd had eyes only for her. She stood, her eyes spitting fire. She was several inches shorter than Lynnette, but was more everything else. More beautiful, more poised, more elegantly dressed, more everything.

"No, not really." Kenny stated, We've just happened to be in the same places at the same time a few times. We have a mutual acquaintance." Kenny hid his grin at Ricco's small eye roll. He loved when she did that. Turning to Lynnette, he began introductions, "Lynnette this is Naricco Maki." Ricco extended her hand. Lynnette looked as if it was a dead fish and shook it like it was one as well.

"Well aren't you a tiny little thing."

Before Ricco could respond, Kenny freed himself from Lynnette's clutches and pulled Ricco into an affectionate hug. In her ear he whispered. "You can't fillet her in front of all these people." Kenny thought he heard a little giggle, but was too caught off guard by the brief moment she gave into the hug. She pulled away. Had he imagined the warmth? Was he so turned around by her beauty, scent, and the scotch that it felt as if she was glad to see him. He wanted to ask her about it, but the moment was gone.

Kenny resisted the urge to lift Lynnette's chin to close her mouth. Instead he said to Ricco, "Naricco, as usual it is a pleasure to see you. You are gorgeous as always, but tonight you are…I would say simply stunning, but there is nothing simple about you. You are indeed a vision."

She stared for a moment before she seemed to gather herself. "Thank you, Mr. Cavanaugh. I should be surprised to see you, but somehow I am not." She turned to Lynnette. "How long have the two of you known each other?"

Kenny was surprised that she cared, but was also thrilled that she did. The question went unanswered as everyone was asked to take their seats by the evening's emcee. Kenny took the seat beside Ricco, much to her displeasure, but Kenny was certain she didn't want to sit next to his cat-loving-empty-headed date. There was an announcement that dinner was being served.

"What the hell are you doing here, Cavanaugh!" Ricco whispered harshly in his ear. He turned from Lynnette's chatter and saw a bright sweet smile on Ricco's face, but the fire in her eyes made him want to toss her over his shoulder, carry her out of there, and kiss her until she melted like ice cream on a hot summer day.

"I was invited, same as you, I assume."

"Lynnette?" She smirked and cocked her head to the side. "I expected better of you."

That she expected anything at all from him was thrilling. Kenny glanced at John deep in conversation with the gentleman at his side, most likely a fellow firefighter, based on the uniform.

"Touché darling."

She rolled her eyes at that and Lynnette snagged his attention.

Throughout dinner, Ricco pointedly ignored him. That was fine, because he paid attention to everything she did, who she talked to, and how much she'd interacted with John. When the dancing started, John wanted her to dance, but she politely declined

Idiot.

Didn't he know the songs were much too fast for her? As to not appear rude, Kenny danced with his date a couple of times, but his eyes never strayed far from Ricco. Lynnette was too self-absorbed to notice.

Finally, seated at the table alone with Ricco, she asked him, "So what are you really doing here? Did Kyle make you come to keep an eye on me?"

"Why would he do that?"

"He's been hovering like a big brother and for some reason he doesn't like John."

"Kyle said that?" Of course Kenny knew that. Kyle, like him, was suspicious of John.

"He doesn't have to. So, what are you really doing here, because I know you have no interest in that bobble you've been parading around in here."

He tried not to show his amusement, because she may just sock him. "I don't?"

"Give me some credit here. I have eyes and yours are everywhere but on her. So what gives?

"Dance with me and I'll tell you." She rolled her eyes for the millionth time of the night. "I promise I'll tell you." She hesitated. He figured she was testing the sincerity of his words. A new song started. It was a song he liked and more importantly, it was nice and slow. "I won't bite and I'll tell you why I'm here." He could tell she wanted to object, but couldn't resist. She finally held out her hand like a royal duchess and Kenny escorted her out to the dance floor walking on a cloud.

Kenny eased her close to his chest like many of the couples on the floor and they began to move like they'd been dancing together all their lives.

"Are you OK?" He asked. Concerned about the tempo of the dance. He knew her breathing wasn't back to normal and that even talking tired her out. "This isn't too strenuous?"

"No, I'm fine." She glanced up at him. "Well?"

"I'm here, Naricco, because I thought I may get a chance to hold you in my arms again."

Chapter 10

Now why the hell did he have to say that?

"I don't believe you and why would I?"

"Because it's true." She rolled her eyes. What frustrated her the most was she wanted to believe him, wanted to be swept away by Kenny and be completely blinded by his electric eyes. The subtle sway, encircled in his arms, could have been her undoing, but she refused to be taken in by his charm, his good looks, his masculine scent, and the illusion of his safety. Her head was starting to spin.

"May I speak with you privately?"

"Huh?"

Her heart fluttered just thinking about being alone with him. That was definitely not a good idea.

"You're speaking to me privately right now."

He looked around. *No, I mean without prying ears.* She looked around and saw John dancing with Lynnette on the other side of the dance floor.

"It's important. I promise," he urged. "no tricks."

She nodded. Walking her out of the ballroom, the warmth of his palm on the small of her back sent more than a tingle through her. They had to walk a ways to find some privacy and she was thankful to sit for a while. The evening was beginning to take its toll on her. She looked up at him and was immediately snared by the intensity of his gaze.

Her brows went up, expectantly. "Well?"

"I know this may be difficult for you to talk about, but can you tell me about the night of the fire."

That was not what she was expecting him to say. She relaxed by leaning back on the beautifully upholstered chair. "It wasn't a traumatic experience. I don't remember anything about it. I was going through the prep list and expected numbers for the pastries and coffee and fell asleep at the desk. When I woke up, I was in the hospital with a tube down my throat."

She saw him wince and wondered the cause. "You alright?"

"Yes."

"Is that it?"

"Will you tell me what happened that led you to be there alone."

"I've been there most evenings alone while we've been getting ready for the grand opening." Again, she saw something cross his face. This time it appeared to be irritation. Ricco stifled the eye roll she wanted to give him. "Anyway," she began again with a little irritation of her own, "the delivery guy was late, so we were all waiting around until he arrived."

"When does he normally arrive?"

"It's difficult to say, because we'd yet established a routine of how much of what we'll need and when. The Boston location will produce the products for the commercial business and the local store."

"I see."

She wasn't sure if he really did understand how much goods that encompassed, but she continued her story. "After we'd inventoried the items and put them all away, we took out the trash. I noticed the cardboard recycle was closer to the building than it usually was, so I ran up to the office to make a note to call the waste management company. We put too much cardboard in there for it to be so close to the building. I got distracted by some emails. One of the guys called up saying they were finished and were leaving."

"So you don't know if they actually locked up or not?"

"I had no reason to think they wouldn't. We take security very seriously. The entire staff was there that night—eleven of us. The guys especially would have made sure to lock up with me left in the store."

She took a few slow breaths and lifted a hand. "Just need a second."

"I'm sorry. I don't mean to exhaust you."

With a gentle shake of her head she responded, "No, I'm fine. Just hadn't talked this much at one time, in a while."

He leaned back and watched a couple walk past them. She took a moment to fill her eyes with him. He was cleanly shaven, which was not his customary look. Normally he sported just a hint of a salt and pepper shadow on his chin and jaw. It matched his hair and vivid silver eyes. He wore a black on black tuxedo. The contrast of his hair and the tux was striking. Kenny Cavanaugh was sexy as sin framed in an edge of danger. He'd literally taken her breath away when she'd spotted him.

Her eyes took a slow journey back up to his face. Caught checking him out, she couldn't even be irritated by the sparkle in his eyes that told her he knew exactly what she was up to. "You know, I've told all of this to the police."

"I'm not the police."

"Why do you even care?"

He looked offended by her words and she was immediately contrite. "That was mean to say. I'm sorry."

"No apologies necessary."

"Anyway, the locks would not have mattered, the fire didn't need a key to get in. Maybe one of the guys threw a cigarette butt in the recycle container. It was full of cardboard. Unlikely, because I don't think any of them smoke, but the container must have caught fire, because there was a new one when I stopped by the shop, yesterday. And it was much farther away than the other one. Come to think of it, we were all surprised it was so close, but didn't think anything of it. We were just glad we didn't have to walk too far to throw away so many boxes"

His forehead creased. "Why do you think it was a new one?"

"It was blue, the other one had been green."

He raised a brow, but did not comment.

"I probably need to be getting back. I'm sure John is looking for me and I've been very rude by leaving for so long."

"Have I told you how beautiful you look tonight?"

Caught off guard by the abrupt question, she answered in her native language. "Hai." She smiled shyly. Too charming for his own good. Or rather, too charming for her own good. "Not in those words, but yes." She bowed slightly, "Arigatou gozaimasu."

"And that means?"

"It is a polite way to say, thank you."

The soft smile on his face touched her in places that caused her to feel fragile and vulnerable.

"How are you, Naricco?"

Why did he have to say her name like that? He said it like he loved the taste of it on his tongue and the sound of it passing through his lips.

How was she?

When finally answered, her words came out as soft and thin as the petal of a cherry blossom. "Okagesama de genki desu." She bowed slightly, again. "It is the equivalent to you saying, 'I'm fine thank you for asking,' but my grandmother would say it means, 'because of you, I am well.' Basically, because you have asked about me, I am well."

He blinked and took in a deep breath. "I am glad."

He reached for her hand and held it gently.

Why did he have to smell so damn good? It took every bit of her willpower not to give in and just be swept away by all that was Kenny Cavanaugh. But after a while her mind began to remember another time she felt safe, and comforted by this man. The very next day, instead of comforted, she felt confused and empty.

And angry.

Very angry.

Ricco wouldn't lie to herself. She wanted this. She wanted the closeness of him. The comfort of his touch. She wanted him to promise her everything would be well. She wanted to want this man, but she couldn't.

The hurt on the other end would be too acute—too damaging.

She didn't want to really know, but couldn't keep herself from asking, "Did you really want to hold me again?" She would pluck her eyes out if she reacted to his response.

"Yes I did, Naricco."

"Why don't you ever call me Ricco."

"I love your name."

"Why?"

"It's beautiful."

"No, why did you want to hold me again?"

"Because you are beautiful. You make me feel whole." He voiced the statements so succinctly she held his eyes for a few moments. Just long enough to not get struck by the electric currents flickering in them. "Then why did you—" She didn't finish; she couldn't ask again why he tossed her away so effortlessly.

"I need to go. I need to get back to my date now and you, yours." She had more questions, because she didn't believe his answer for a moment. She would ask no more questions. His answers would not answer the call of her need. They wouldn't answer the heartache she carried like a weight for the loss of her parents and his answers would do nothing to quell the sting of rejection stabbing her every movement.

Ricco found John still on the dance floor, with someone else this time. She feigned more exhaustion than she really had and asked him to bring her home. John tried more than once to get her to let him inside her home, but she refused, telling him again that she just needed to rest.

By the time she turned to lock her door, she was shaking. Ricco took out her phone, tapped Symphony's number, and prayed her friend would agree to her plan.

"Hey."

"Everything OK? You sound weird."

"Yes, I'm fine."

"Did you have a good time tonight? I figured you'd be home early, but you couldn't have been there more than an hour. Are you sure everything's alright?"

Instead of answering Symphony's question she said, "I think I'll take you up on your offer." Ricco tried to hold in the sob, but couldn't. There was a pause on the phone—Ricco loved Symphony. She didn't ask any questions, just waited for her friend to tell her what was going on.

"OK, so I'm not so fine." She said at the end of the sob.

"When do you want to go?"

"As soon as possible."

"Are you certain?"

"Yes, I promise I'll be fine. Just promise me you and Kyle won't tell anyone where I am."

When Ricco got the answer she wanted, she clicked off the phone and began to pack.

Chapter 11

Kenny walked into the spacious foyer and released a loud whistle. The house was unbelievable. He figured Terry's aunt and uncle paid at least six million for it. The estate was located on a semi-private island accessible only by boat. There was only one other house located on it. He considered that pretty private in his book.

When he talked to Terry about wanting to get away for a while, Terry offered him to stay at his uncle Dixon's place while he and his wife were on an extended stay in Europe. When the person they'd commissioned to house sit canceled at the last minute, they were in need of a new candidate. Kenny had met Dixon while he was visiting his sons in Boston. They'd gotten along great, so Dixon was more than happy to allow Kenny to stay at their home for as long as he needed. They were just glad not to have it sitting empty for so long.

The house itself had six bedrooms. There were two sets of garages. Why so much garage space on an island, he had no idea, but he figured it was where they kept their toys. Golf carts, jet skis, and such. Terry told him that each garage had an apartment above it. He planned on staying in one of those, but wanted to check out the main house before he settled in.

He whistled again. The architecture was remarkable. From where he stood in the foyer, he could see the pool, boat dock, and party deck out back. He imagined the nice breeze that flowed through if the front and back doors were open. Kenny imagined sitting on the deck with Naricco. Would she enjoy the view? What would they talk about? She'd surprised him and talked to him at the ball, but he knew the exact moment when the hurt snaked its way around her heart again.

Would he ever be able to have her?

She nearly died in that fire.

The fire.

Kyle told him there was more smoke and water damage than damage from actual flames. Most of the fire damage was on the outside of the structure. Had it been the dumpster. Did someone toss something in it to cause the fire? He knew for certain that no other business in the neighborhood had the green dumpsters. Why had there been a green one near Symphony's and why so close to the building. The garbage truck would have to do some fancy maneuvering to get to it. More importantly, why had it been deemed an electrical fire?

Winter Lightning

Kenny didn't know the answers to those questions, but he would keep searching until he found them. His thoughts turned back to Ricco. He wasn't ashamed to admit that on the night of the ball, jealousy burned him from the inside out. She was so beautiful and he didn't trust that damn fireman.

He felt like a lunatic stalker, passing in front of her condo to make sure the fireman wasn't there. He'd had to practically shove Lynnette in her door, close it, and damn near sprint back to his car. She wasn't too happy about him not going in for a drink and had called him and voiced her displeasure over the phone. He half listened as he pretty much cut the corners on two wheels trying to get to Ricco's place, which was about fifteen minutes from Lynnette's.

Lynette was none too pleased when he announced he was ready to leave the ball. He said there was an emergency at one of his sites and had to go. She wasn't ready. He told her she could either leave with him and he'd see her home or he would come back to pick her up after he checked on the site. She opted for the former.

There was a tinge of guilt for using her to go to the ball, but she'd gotten a few good meals out of it. The woman was hateful, not too bright and, basically dull brass compared to Ricco.

Kenny's phone distracted him from his musings.

"Do you have any information for me, Cliff?"

"It's not good."

"What is it?"

"Casey had Tony—"

"Tony from the bureau?" He cut him off.

"Yeah, he took a look at the device that was attached to your truck." Kenny waited. He knew Tony was the best explosive guy in the business. "And?"

"And it's sophisticated stuff. This shit wasn't made in someone's garage, it was developed in a lab. A secure lab."

Kenny let the weight of this new revelation sink in. Just as he figured, all this shit had been tied to his past. "What other intel do we have? Is Ricco a target or, were they trying to destroy my reputation, because I'd done the work on the structure?"

"So far, it looks like she was just caught up in your mess." That allowed him a modicum of comfort. "But Kenny…"

"Yeah? Whoever is doing this wants to hurt you bad, man. I'm pretty sure if they knew you were into someone, that they'd use her to hurt you at any cost. Especially after what happened with—" Cliff didn't finish his statement. It was well known that that subject was off limits. Kenny walked to the back of the house and looked out. He knew Cliff was right. "You still there?"

"I'm here."

"It may not be a bad idea for you to sneak away for a while until we get all this stuff lined out."

"I'm already ahead of you."

"Is that why you didn't answer from your other phone?" Kenny had a phone that was completely secure from being traced or hacked.

"Yes. Anyone who needs to contact me, knows how."

"Ok, man. Keep your head down and we'll find this prick as soon as we can. I think we're getting close to a breakthrough.

"Ok, Cliff. You know how to reach me. I still want the team to keep an eye on Symphony's for a little while longer and Ricco."

"You got it."

He clicked off the phone. Kenny planned on using his time away to get to the bottom of all the sabotage he'd been experiencing. He knew better than to go to the police. If that device was created where he suspected it was, then this would have to be another black ops mission.

This was exactly what Ricco needed—solitude, water, and the Carolina sun warming her face. The soft sway of the porch swing lulled her into a relaxed state that she'd not experienced in some time.

She was at the home that was willed to Symphony after the death of her aunt. Ricco had fallen in love with it when she'd come to Symphony and Kyle's wedding. It was a spacious cottage with the kitchen of her dreams. Symphony's aunt had been a baker as well. Mr. Jenkins, the man who kept up the place, had already come, stocked the pantry and fridge with any and everything she would want or need. She could cater a banquet if she wanted to. But all she'd had energy to do was unpack, eat a sandwich, and collapse on the porch swing

Ricco remembered she hadn't yet called Symphony to let her know she was all settled. Retrieving her phone, she pushed the number for Symphony and before she could get a word out, Symphony rushed in to say, "What's wrong?"

"Why would you think something's wrong?"

"I wasn't expecting to hear from you until later. I figured it would take you a while to get from the airport."

"I'm fine. All in one piece." The words just barely a whisper because she was so exhausted.

"Fridge and everything stocked?"

"Yes, but I already feel like I'm taking advantage of you, since you're still paying me while I'm sitting on my butt."

"You were pulled from a fire, in my bakery, just barely alive. It is the *least* we can do."

Ricco wanted to say more, but she knew it would do no good. "I know it won't do any good to argue with you. You're about as stubborn as I am."

"You're absolutely correct." Neither spoke for a few beats. "Are you ready to tell me about it?"

"About what?"

"About what has you running scared. I know it has to be more than the fire. Though, it may have been traumatic, you've faced worse." And she had. "So what is it?"

"Didn't you offer me an opportunity to recuperate out here?"

"Naricco Maki, please give me more credit than you are. You turned me down more than a few times. Even though I know it's a bit isolated down there, I felt that the fresh air and quiet would be good for you. Plus it would put you several states away from this bakery." Symphony rushed on, "And before you say anything, I can't wait to have you back at work, but I will not have you back at the risk of your health. I

113

know you too well, Ricco. You would be stopping by here all the time, so yes, I offered you my place there, but you adamantly refused." Ricco was about to say something, "I'm not done." Ricco shut her mouth. "So, I'm going to ask you again, Naricco Maki, are you ready to tell me what has you running scared?"

Ricco sighed. She was sure the two-word reply would be a sufficient answer. "Kenny Cavanaugh."

Chapter 12

"Are you certain you'll be OK here?"

"Yes, Mr. Kenny. I'm not afraid."

He couldn't help the smile when he heard her call him Mr. Kenny. She was the only person who'd ever called him that. Kenny hated to leave her, but he had no choice."

"Ok. Just stay hidden and don't make a sound. I will be back to get you as soon as I can. Do you remember how I taught you to count the minutes?" Her head bobbed up and down. Her chubby little face was dirty and scratched from when she'd fallen from the car. "I will be back in ten minutes. If I'm not, do you remember where I told you to run?" Her head bobbed again.

"I'm not afraid, Mr. Kenny." She said again.

Kenny smiled at her show of strength. She was the bravest little girl he knew. He touched the scar along her jawline. "OK, my little warrior, start counting.

"One Mississippi, two Mississippi…" She paused and he paused.

"What's wrong?"

"What's a Mississippi?"

Smiling again, he said, "It is the name of a place in my country and the name of a long river."

She nodded firmly and began her counting again.

Kenny ran as fast as he could to the shadows of the aged vacant building across the street. All the nearby buildings were vacant and decaying. He turned to give one final look at the structure where his charge was concealed for the moment. He needed to hurry, complete the mission, and get back to her. She could not go with him into the danger he faced.

Kenny took a deep breath and turned away. He closed his eyes and offered a prayer that she would be safe until he returned. He did not see the night sky light up. Momentarily deafened by the blast, Kenny was lifted and hurled through the glass of an ancient store window. His world moved in slow motion as he placed hands over his ears to try and stop the ringing blaring in his head. He could not even hear his own screams ripping from him.

After what seemed like an eternity, Kenny was finally able to rise from the bed of glass and debris littered around him, oblivious to the pieces lodged in his skin. The building across the street was engulfed in flames.

"Frances!" He screamed. "Frances!" Struggling to run towards the flames, another blast lifted and flung him again.

Kenny cried out and jolted upright in bed. His heart raced; it always did after he relived that night in his dreams. It took him a moment to realize where he was or rather where he wasn't. He was no longer in his worst nightmare. He'd never forgiven himself for failing her and never would.

It was morning. Kenny shook off the last dregs of the dream and walked over to the window. From the position of the sun, it appeared to be later in the morning than he was used to getting up, even when he slept in. Trying to refocus on the present, he marveled at the beauty of the estate. It was nestled and a bit hidden among the trees if you came at it from the front or sides. Of course the back was free of trees to enjoy the water views. The apartment he occupied was in the front allowing him to enjoy the wooded area. If he could choose anywhere he wanted to live, he'd pick a place like this, though his home didn't lack much in view and comforts. This place was in a wooded area and had the advantage being on the water. It was two vacations in one.

The ringing of his phone moved him back towards the bed. He picked it up knowing it was Cliff. "What's up Cliff?"

"We found something but we don't know what it is."

"What do you mean?" Kenny walked back to the window.

"We think it's some kind of coded message. Do you have the encrypted fax machine with you?"

"Yeah. Send it to me and I'll take a look."

"To us, it just looks like a page full of numbers, but I have a hunch that there's more to it."

Kenny was about to ask how Cliff had gotten the information, but something a few yards away caught his attention.

"What was that, Kenny? I didn't catch what you said."

Kenny blinked several times and looked again where he'd seen the movement. "Kenny!"

Cliff's voice startled him. He was apparently still shaken from the dream. He looked again and a flock of birds took flight. For a moment, he thought he'd seen a woman. A woman who looked a lot like Ricco. It wasn't unusual for him to see Frances's face on a child he spotted in a crowd. The first time it happened. He was almost arrested. He'd scared the hell out of the little girl and her mother. He figured since he hadn't been able to get Ricco off his mind, he was seeing visions of her now.

"Kenny?" Cliff sounded concerned.

"I'm here, man. Just got distracted by some birds outside the window." He sat heavily in a chair, frustrated with his afflicted conscience. "Send me the stuff. I'm not sure how much help I can be, but I'll give it a shot." He clicked off the call.

His stomach let him know that it was well past his normal breakfast time. So, he went into the bathroom to get cleaned up. There was a bottle of perfume he'd not noticed yesterday. The bottle, a beautiful cut crystal in the shape of a globe. The stopper took the form of an intricate lotus flower. He popped the stopper free and the fragrance filled him with a familiar scent.

"This smells like Ricco." He spoke aloud. Oh he was really losing it. Not only was he seeing her, he was smelling her as well. Shaking his head, he put the perfume back on the counter and headed back in the bedroom area in search of some shorts and a T-shirt.

Dr. Harley told Ricco that walking would build up her strength and help with her breathing, so she decided to take a walk after she prepared herself some eggs. It was just about all she could do on her own right now. Later, Mr. Jenkins, whom she'd found out from Symphony was the gentleman friend of Symphony's late aunt Helen, would bring her a prepared dinner for the next couple of days.

Her breathing was improving a lot, but she still got exhausted quickly. She wanted to get well as fast as possible. The walk would do her good.

Almost to their home, Ricco remembered, too late, Symphony telling her that Dixon and Gloria Phoenix were out of town for a while. When Ricco had come for Symphony's wedding, she'd stayed with the couple as one of their guests. She'd been in charge of the wedding cake and had baked it in their fabulous state of the art kitchen.

She was tired. The walk cost her more energy than she had to give. Without thinking if they had a house sitter or not, she figured since she was already there, she'd just rest on the back patio until she had enough strength to walk back to the cottage. The house itself was armed with an elaborate alarm system, but there were no fences since the island was private, so she just walked around by the pool and stretched out on the chaise. Before long, the sun lulled her to sleep.

Kenny frowned at the papers coming from the fax machine. He was pretty good at deciphering code, but he couldn't get a grasp on the numbers filling the page Cliff sent him. There was no consistent pattern that made any sense. The only thing he noticed was that each line contained seventy-five numbers. He was sure something was there. But what?

A slight headache pressed against his forehead. He needed coffee and food. The sleeping area was separated by a partial wall and on the other side, there was a very comfortable seating area with a television as well as the kitchen. For a guest apartment, the kitchen was large with all the amenities a person needed in a kitchen. It was stocked. They must've done it for the house sitter they'd expected, because the fridge and pantry held all the items he needed to make a large breakfast and a nice pot of coffee.

Kenny spotted some King Arthur flour and immediately had a taste for Molly biscuits. There was also baking powder, and real butter. He popped the unsalted butter in the freezer while he gathered all the ingredients. If the butter was very hard, he could grate it instead of cutting it with a pastry blender.

Kenny learned at an early age how to make biscuits from scratch. One morning, when he was ten, for Mother's Day, he wanted to surprise his mom and bring her breakfast in bed. He'd had no money to buy her a gift, but he'd seen a recipe for biscuits on the back of a bag of flour and decided that's what he'd give his mom as a gift—a homemade breakfast. She'd been so surprised and pleased that cooking for her soon became part of his routine.

She couldn't cook at all—just never had the knack for it. So, he started collecting cookbooks, finding most of them at thrift stores, and anytime he saw one on the back of a package, he either cut it out or wrote it down.

Even after he'd moved out, he still cooked for his mother. Not as often, but at least twice during the week and every Sunday they had a big meal together. She came over right after church. His doorbell rang at one twenty in the afternoon, like clockwork. They had the biscuits every Sunday. He'd perfected the biscuits over the years, learning new tricks like freezing the butter a bit and grating it instead of cutting it through with a pastry blender

Kenny's thirty-third birthday and Mother's Day fell on the same day that year. The biscuits were hot and ready. It wasn't until the doorbell did not ring at the anticipated time that he realized something was wrong. She was never late—for anything.

His mother never arrived.

The biscuits went untouched that year. At fifty-eight, she'd died peacefully in her sleep, the night before. She had not been ill and there was no sign of heart disease or anything else. She simply did not wake up. She was the only family he'd ever had.

It had been just over a year since he lost his mother. He missed her. He missed her laugh, her smile, her horrible cooking.

Kenny missed his mom.

From the time he could remember, they were the best of friends. His dad had died right before he was born, so it was just his mom and him. She was the one who taught him how to be a man. She'd taught him everything. Well…except how to cook. And he loved her still.

Last month on Mother's Day, he'd made the biscuits. It was the first time since his last birthday. They were the best batch he'd ever made. Maybe it was a sign that his mom wanted him to keep making her biscuits, so whenever he got the opportunity, he made them.

His Molly Biscuits.

Molly Cavanaugh was the greatest woman he'd ever known. Whatever he wanted, all he simply had to do was ask. He knew that about her, loved that about her, but he never asked for much nor did he ask often.

She'd given him everything he needed. The least he could do was give her her very own biscuits.

All his men loved when he made Molly biscuits and brought them to a site.

Molly biscuits, honey, and butter were like nectar of the gods. Kenny's stomach growled as he began to mix the ingredients. He thought about the beautiful scenery out back and looked forward to enjoying his breakfast on the patio when he was done. His mother would have loved this place. She loved the coast. It didn't matter which one. She just loved being on the water.

He realized then that something had changed inside of him. He used to try not to think of his mother, because it made him so sad, now he realized that although he missed her terribly, the memories made him feel a little closer to her. He was certain she watched over him.

Kenny found the bed tray that decorated the foot of the bed when he arrived and wondered if it was placed there, because guests liked to take their meals out back. He placed the papers from Cliff, his breakfast, coffee, and a bottle of water on the tray and made his way, to the main house and out back.

His thoughts somehow found their way to Ricco knowing his mother would have liked her.

Kenny wondered what she was doing and if the fireman was still snooping around. A fissure of irritation tightened his jaw just thinking about the man. Hating to have left her so far out of reach, he said a silent prayer to ask his mom to keep Ricco safe just as he was certain she did for him. He then stepped out into the late morning sunshine; the sun feeling glorious on his face. He needed this. Needed the time away to figure out some things.

From his initial tour when he'd arrived, he knew the patio was separated into two covered sections. One side held the loungers and the other an outside dining area. He opened the door, held it open wide with his hip to bring the tray through, and headed to the dining table.

A shift in the wind picked up one of the sheets of paper from the tray. He quickly put the tray down on the table, careful not to jostle his coffee too much, so he could catch it before it landed in the pool. He turned quickly to grab it, but the wind forced it farther away from him. The document ended up plastered against the bottom of one of the patio French doors. He stooped to grab it and stopped in his tracks.

There was someone lying on the chaise. He reached for his Glock he normally had tucked near the small of his back in a concealed carry belt around his

waist, but realized he had put it on this morning.
Before irritation of being so careless set in, he noticed
that the person appeared to be asleep.

Kenny carefully stepped towards the chaise and
his breath caught.

How was—

How?

His mind could not form a cohesive answer to
the question that came to him. How was this possible?
His heart slammed in his chest. He thought about the
dream that had woke him earlier and wondered if in
fact he was awake at all.

How was it possible that Naricco was right
here? He'd just asked his mom to keep her safe. The
wind gently caressed his face and the document floated
to his feet. Kenny reached to grab it and whispered,
"Are you sure about this, mom?"

"Yes, Kenny. Please…"

The reply came from Ricco. Her words horse
and a bit labored. He stepped closer to her and saw her
turn from her back to her side. She pulled her knees
towards her chest. "Thank you for holding me."

It was what she'd said that night he'd held her
in her hotel room right before she'd drifted off to sleep.

Why was she saying it now? Was she dreaming? He thought again. And most importantly, how did she get here and why was she here?

Chapter 13

Her head nestled in the crook of his neck, the strength of his arms surrounding her, and his promise that everything would be OK, was the best part of a perfect world that she'd ever known.

"May I stay?" He asked.

"Yes, Kenny. Please." She replied. She noticed that the words didn't hurt nor was it difficult to breathe. "Thank you for holding me. It's just what I needed. How did you know?"

Ricco couldn't get enough of his scent. It was subtle, yet intoxicating. She inhaled deeply.

Her chest burned. The deep breath caused a wracking cough. She clutched her throat, trying to grab some air and unable to get as much as she needed. The cough snatched her from the dream faster than she was ready to break from it.

She hated waking up crazy with a racing heart. Tears ran down her face from the cough. She wiped them away and opened her eyes. Ricco startled before she remembered she was on Gloria and Dixon's patio. She coughed again, wiping more tears. "Shit!" She spit out the word between coughing fits. "When will this end?"

"Are you OK?"

She turned towards the question faster than she should have. The coughing seized her again, but through the coughs and tears she saw a pair of legs in cargo shorts. Panic gripped her.

Who the hell—

She wanted to sit up but couldn't at the moment.

"Naricco…take it easy. Try to take slow shallow breaths."

Naricco? Only one person called her by her full name. Was she losing her mind?

Still asleep?

How was Kenny Cavanaugh standing on the Phoenixes' porch?

Looking up confirmed that it was indeed him standing right in front of her.

"What are you doing here?" She asked when she finally gathered enough oxygen to form the words.

"What are you doing here?" She heard him ask.

She slowly stood and placed her arms on her head hoping it would ease the coughing. He reached to assist her, but when she held up a hand to stay him, he hesitated. Seemingly resigned that he could be of no help to her, she watched Kenny calmly take a seat on the chaise she'd just vacated.

Briefly, she wondered if he'd followed her there, but then remembered his look of genuine surprise to see her. It took her a few moments to get herself together. Using her shirt to wipe away the tears, she prayed the coughing would give her a break long enough to find out what was going on and what in the world had brought Kenny Cavanaugh to the same island she'd escaped to. This could not possibly be a coincidence.

"Sit, Naricco."

Her mind was too befuddled to come up with a flippant comeback, so she simply sat. The eyebrow easing up her forehead asked her question again.

He had the nerve to smirk.

"You're like winter lightning."

"Pardon me?" That smirk again.

She hadn't meant to say the words out loud, but there they were out in the atmosphere, unable to be stuffed back into her mouth.

"Unexpected." She answered him. The coughing started again and she was so damn frustrated that she couldn't have a simple conversation without damn near dying. She hadn't felt this way since right out of the hospital. She could only assume it was the long walk and being startled awake that ignited the coughing fit.

"Would you like for me to get you a glass of water?"

Hand over her mouth, eyes watering, she shook her head no. It took a moment more before she could speak again. "I just want to know what you're doing here."

"I'm house sitting, but I want to know more about this winter lightning."

She ignored the second part of his statement. "I know that Gloria and Dixon are out of town, but why would Kenny Cavanaugh of Cavanaugh Construction be house sitting?"

"I needed to get away."

"Did you know I was here?"

"It is a delightful surprise, Naricco." Oh how she loved the way he said her name—slow, strong, and steady. "But no, I did not know you were here. Did you know I was here?"

"Of course not!"

"Take it easy."

She caught herself before she sucked in too much air too fast. "No, Kenny, I didn't know you were here."

"Then what are you doing here?"

"I asked you first."

"Actually, we asked at the same time, but since you are here on the patio of a house I'm in charge of, I think I deserve an answer."

She rolled her eyes, before looking away. "I fell asleep."

"I gathered that, but how did you end up on a patio on a private island?"

"Semi-private." He lifted a brow and his eyes danced with intrigue. "My doctor said I needed exercise."

"Long walk from Boston."

Was he mocking her? "I walked from Symphony's place. I thought I'd come see Dixon and Gloria to let them know I was here, but when I got here, I remembered they were out of town. By that time, I was too exhausted to walk back. So, I walked around here to rest. I guess I fell asleep."

"Symphony's place?"

"Yes, she owns the other half of the island."

"She does?"

"You didn't know?"

"No, Terry never mentioned it." He frowned. "Seems odd that she would own a place where his family lived."

"It was totally by coincidence. Her aunt left it to her after she died."

"Oh."

"You never answered my question." She asked him.

"Neither did you."

Ricco decided to be completely honest with him. "I came out here to recuperate in peace."

"In peace?"

"Yes, Kenny. I was afraid you would come over again." She gathered her knees to her chest and leaned back against the chaise. "You showed up twice in one day." She hit her fist on the cushion, emphasizing her last words. She heard him about to say something, but he stopped when she continued. "Kenny, the day I met you, you made me feel safe, wanted, and it was the first time I hadn't felt alone in a very long time."

"Naricco—"

"I delayed my flight back to Florida so I could spend just a little while longer with you." Ricco's eyes were on the ornate blades of the ceiling fan above her, because she didn't dare look at the pity in his eyes. She was pathetic. "And after such a wonderful time, you sent me a text," she let out a gruff laugh, "a freaking text." She took in a slow shallow breath. "You sent me a text to tell me that it wouldn't be a good idea for us to see each other again. So we didn't. Not personally, anyway."

"Naricco."

She ignored him. "And when I had to see you about the shop, you would never believe that one night you'd chased all my fears away." She felt his hand on her knee and his touch seared her. She moved her knee and he had sense enough to pull his hand away. "So, to answer your question of what I'm doing here, Mr. Cavanaugh, I came here to get away from you." She chuckled again. It hurt her chest. "Lots of good that did." She sat up, no longer ashamed of her feelings or the tears glazing her eyes. "If you're not here, because you knew I was here, then why are you here, Kenny?"

"I'm here, because someone tried to kill me outside of your apartment, the other day, and I figured if I was far away from you, you'd stay safe."

Ricco was not sure what she was expecting him to say, but that sure was not it.

Her mind reeling. "Start from the beginning." Because surely there had to be a beginning and she wanted to...no, needed to hear it.

He nodded.

She waited.

Chapter 14

"First, let me clear up something."

The sadness in her eyes was slowly killing him. He'd put that look there and he hated himself for it. "I haven't been able to get you off my mind since the first moment I saw you. I know it sounds cliché, but it's the truth."

"It doesn't sound cliché at all."

"I'm sorry I treated you so horribly."

"And second?"

"Second?"

"If there is a first, there must be a second."

Before he could speak, his stomach growled loudly. She lifted a brow. "I'd come out to eat my breakfast."

"Eat."

He was going to brush her off, but the noise coming from his stomach begged for food. "Join me. I have plenty. I'll just pop it in the microwave for a minute and grab another plate. By the time you make your way to the table, I'll be back with breakfast."

"Ha. Ha." She retorted, dryly.

"Join me?"

"Sure. Why not?" Kenny helped her up. "Go on and get the plate. I'm hungry too."

He went ahead of her, grabbed the plate and ran into the house. It didn't take him long to find what he needed while the food was heating. When Kenny returned to the table, Ricco was seated and looking at one of the pages he had stuck underneath the tray.

"What is this?" 'She waved the sheet before tucking it back under the tray.

Kenny placed the plates and extra silverware on the table and began scooping food onto the empty plate. The biscuits were steaming in a little basket he'd found in the guest apartment. "I don't know yet."

"Why do you have it?"

"I'm trying to figure out if it contains some sort of code."

"Are you a code talker?" She asked as she stuffed a small bite of eggs in her mouth. "You cooked this?"

Kenny wasn't sure if he should be offended or not, but he sure was enjoying a Ricco who wasn't glaring at him. He ignored the first question, not really wanting to give her an answer. "Yes, I cooked this."

She picked up a biscuit and pulled it apart. "Kenny Cavanaugh you did not make this biscuit!" She sounded so harmless. Her voice was just above a whisper, but he knew better. He knew better than to underestimate her bite.

"Those are my specialty—Molly biscuits."

"Molly biscuits?"

"Yes, they were named for my mom. They were her favorite."

"Were?"

"Yes, she died a little more than a year ago."

"I'm sorry, Kenny." The sincerity in her words touched him.

"Here. Slather them with butter and drown them in honey."

To his surprise and delight, she did exactly that. He couldn't put into words how pleased he was watching her enjoy his cooking. He knew after her earlier coughing fit that he shouldn't try to encourage too much conversation.

He finished well before her because of the small bites she was forced to take. She didn't seem to mind. He figured the surprise of how good the food was, kept her mind occupied, rather than paying attention to him.

He sipped his coffee, pretending to study the documents in front of him, while stealing glances of Ricco whenever she wasn't paying attention.

Why was he so drawn to this woman?

137

He didn't know the answer. All he knew was that he was indeed drawn to her and didn't want to do anything about it, except keep her safe and chase all her fears away.

Ricco pushed her empty plate away from her, smiled, and patted her belly. "Mmmm."

Kenny gave her a gallant nod and smiled back. "Glad you enjoyed it." He stood. "Let me get this out of the way." He watched her sit back in the plush chair and look around.

"Beautiful." She breathed. The word came out clear and soft. "I can't get enough of this view."

"Yes. Very beautiful." His eyes never left her. "Me either."

She looked up and found him watching her. He held her eyes. His arms ached to hold her, but instead of going to her and pulling her into them, and risk being throttled with one of the coffee mugs, he gathered the plates to take to the kitchen.

"Let me help." She whispered.

Her voice sounded much weaker. He figured she'd talked more than she needed and was probably in pain. He wondered how far she'd walked, because even after talking to her for a while at the ball she didn't sound this frail.

"No, you sit. I got it." He lifted the tray and the documents shifted across the table. "Will you hold these until I return? I don't want them to fly into the pool."

She nodded and picked them up. "I'm going to…" She took a few deep breaths, "go back to the chaise."

"Need my help getting up?" And to his surprise she extended a hand to him. Why was she so exhausted? After she was on her feet, she took another deep breath. "You got it?"

"Mhmm."

She moved slower now than she had before, but she was steady on her feet. "I think with the travel and walk over here, I've really worn myself out." She said.

Wishing he could help in some way, he just nodded, piled the dishes on the tray and brought them to the kitchen. He decided to go ahead and wash the few dishes in the main house instead of bringing them all the way back to the guest apartment.

He was just drying his hands when his phone buzzed in his pocket. He was surprised Cliff was calling so soon.

"Yeah?"

"That fireman has been snooping around Ms. Maki's condo."

"What do you mean, 'snooping around?'"

"I mean, he's gone to her place twice. Neither time did she let him in. I've seen him driving by a few times and now he's sitting across the street in his car. He's the only person who has been to visit."

"Keep an eye on him. I'm pretty sure he's not on the up and up. I think Kyle may have mentioned that Ricco was staying with Joshua and Alexandra Phoenix for now." Cliff sounded relieved. Through the windows, Kenny saw Ricco looking over the documents. He didn't know why he lied to his friend. He knew he could trust the information with Cliff, but for some reason he just wanted to keep the fact that he was here with Ricco to himself for the moment. He would tell his friend in a few days.

"Is that it?"

"No."

"What else?"

"The fire chief is dead."

Kenny froze. His eyes went instinctively back out to Ricco. "Dead?"

"Yes, I saw it come across the TV not long ago."

"How?"

"The news says it was a car accident."

"You don't believe that?"

"Nope." Kenny waited for him to continue. "He was in the tunnel. There were no cars near him. He just slammed into the wall."

"Toxicology report been released yet?"

"Yep. It was clean. There are some unconfirmed reports that the man was a really bad diabetic."

"Keep me updated."

"Will do, boss."

"Stop calling me that."

Cliff chuckled before clicking off the phone.

The fire chief was dead. What did this mean? He needed to find out how the fire and the bomb fit together—if they did at all.

Kenny walked out to where Ricco sat cross-legged. She was so engrossed in the documents that she hadn't seemed to notice him. He sat on the chaise next to hers.

"Does 'the free one' mean anything to you?" He was sure his face etched with confusion. "These documents. They repeat those three words over and over in all of the documents." She looked up at him. "What is this?"

"How do you know what it says? I could not distinguish any pattern from the numbers there."

"No you wouldn't be able to, but I see numbers differently than most people. It is very easy for me to pick up on subtle patterns."

"I usually can as well, but I couldn't make sense out of it." Could she really have picked up a pattern?

"That's probably because the code words are in Japanese. It is my first language. I tend to form words in my own language, first."

"But these are numbers."

"All characters tell a story, Kenny San." She said the words clear and free of an American accent. For just a moment, she was Naricco Maki, his Japanese beauty. "I've asked you this already and you distracted me with food, so, I will ask you again and I want you to be completely honest with me." He knew what she would ask before she asked it. "What are you doing here? And what did you mean, someone tried to kill you when you left my apartment the other day?"

Kenny wondered if, in fact, she was here because he'd asked his mom to keep her safe, or was she there because he'd asked his mom to keep him safe. At any rate, Kenny was certain they needed each other.

He would tell her everything he could, but he was not ready to share his full story. He could not tell her about Evelyn—not yet.

Chapter 15

"So are you going to answer my questions?"

"I've come here to try to get away while I try to find out who is really behind the sabotage of my company."

"You mean the fires?"

"Among other things."

"I assume you mean the attempt on your life?"

"Yes."

"Why would someone want to kill you? Is the construction business that cut-throat?" She couldn't imagine someone really trying to kill him. Maybe it was just an overactive imagination.

He gave a little chuckle, but his eyes were very serious. "It can be, but I've not always been in construction."

Why was she having to drag out every single thing from him. He was careful to only answer her questions and not elaborate. "What business were you in before construction?"

"I was in the business of liberation."

What did that mean? "Liberation?"

"Yes."

"Kenny, you aren't making any sense."

Strands of her hair blew across her face. He reached up as if to move it and hesitated. "May I?"

All she could do was nod. He slid his hand along her face, capturing the wayward strands and tucking them gently behind her ear.

"You're so beautiful."

She lowered her eyes suddenly feeling shy and vulnerable. Feelings she'd always tried so hard to overcome.

"What do you mean, you were in the business of liberation?" She wanted to get this conversation back on track.

He took in a deep breath, his eyes never leaving hers, For a moment, she thought he wouldn't answer her, but then he said, "People." He stated firmly. "I was in the business of liberating people."

"What people? Liberating them from what?"

"Whomever from whatever."

She wasn't quite sure what her face said to him, but his eyes flashed with anxiousness.

"It almost sounds like you were an assassin." She saw her parents lying on the mat in their sleeping room with bullet holes to their heads. Surely—

"It's not what you're thinking."

"How do you know what I'm thinking?"

"I can tell by the way you're closing up on me, that you're thinking the worst."

"Make me think something else."

"People paid me to remove people from undesirable situations."

"Like hostages?" She needed to know that what he was describing was a noble cause.

"Sometimes, yes."

"Dangerous situations?"

"Yes."

Somewhere in the distance, they heard a boat horn blow. They both looked towards the water as if answers to their unspoken questions floated there.

"Were you always successful?"

"Not always."

"You're thinking that someone from that part of your past, is trying to kill you." If the work he'd done was as dangerous as she'd imagined, there was a real possibility that either because of his failure or success, someone would want revenge. He didn't answer her, because it had not been a question. "You don't like talking about that part of your life, do you?"

"No."

"Why?"

"Because all of it was top secret, it wasn't pleasant, and I was not always successful."

146

She was going to let it go, but still had just a few more questions. "I know you don't like talking about this, but I have a few more questions." He nodded. "Did you work for a government agency or were you a private mercenary?"

"Mercenary?"

"If you didn't work for a government agency, that's the only term I could come up with."

She tried to hold his gaze, but the vividness of his eyes were too much to take in sometimes. "I worked for a government agency, a contractor of sorts, for all my missions except one."

There was something broken in his tone that made her own heart break for him. It was bad. It was really bad and she wasn't sure if she wanted to take on the weight of it. At least not yet.

She wanted to lighten the air between them and visit a more recent past. "One thing that's really been bothering me, is how you knew my phone number that night." There was no need in telling him what night. He knew exactly what night she meant. It was *the* night. The night that had changed her life.

How could one moment heal and break a heart all at once?

"I called in a favor. Now, I realize I may have put you in danger by doing so."

Whoa! That got her attention.

"A favor? From who?"

"A guy I used to work with. I've just recently learned that there may have been a breach in intelligence in one or more of my missions."

"How could getting my phone number put me in danger?"

"They may be under the impression that you're special to me."

And they would be wrong. She, of course, knew that firsthand.

They talked for another hour before her throat was too raw to say another word. Kenny drove her back to the cottage in one of the golf carts in the garage. There were a couple ATVs in there as well, which made them both grin and look forward to another day when she was feeling stronger.

Ricco's mind was too filled with questions for her to get any sleep that night. The only thing that resonated in her mind over and over was, he'd stayed away to try to protect her.

To protect her.

Someone tried to kill him right outside of her condo and his sole purpose for being on the island had been to protect her. That was too incredible to fathom. She remembered his words from her condo.

I am whatever you want me to be, Naricco.

What exactly did she want him to be?

There was still so much mystery surrounding Kenny Cavanaugh—all too incredible to believe, especially after his newest revelations.

Of course, she'd heard about someone making it look like he was trying to intimidate some of the businesses that were being renovated. However, she was shocked when he told her that they were sure the Symphony's fire was an act of arson.

Arson.

Why?

Apparently, this was the same question Kenny wanted answers to. Symphony was new to the neighborhood. Was it her connection to the Phoenixes, the store's connection to Cavanaugh Construction, or could it possibly be Ricco's connection to Kenny?

But how could that be? She'd never spent time with him out in public except that once for lunch and when he'd driven her to the airport. Kenny told her that he used to work briefly for the CIA. From what he'd told her, she got the impression that he was some sort of soldier for hire. She was still trying to reconcile the Kenny of Cavanaugh Construction with Kenny Cavanaugh—soldier for hire.

How had it come to be that they'd both escaped to the same place? Was he being honest with her? Had he really not known she was there? Most importantly, would she ever get the answers to all her questions?

So many questions, but the burning one was where did they go from here?

Chapter 16

They'd been on the island for two weeks.

For two weeks she completely followed the doctor's orders and had to admit that she felt better and stronger. She was also completely in love with Kenny Cavanaugh.

She couldn't help it.

Yes, she'd pushed thoughts of him out of her head after their miserable parting in Boston, but if she was being honest with herself, she'd never really pushed him out of her heart. That very first night, he'd burrowed himself there in the form of hope and a calmness she hadn't experienced in a very long time. Those fragments of Kenny never left her. Which probably explained why she was always quick to fling anger at him.

Something happened over the past two weeks. She found that the anger she held in reserve for him was too much to carry. She didn't worry about the past or fret over the future. She wanted to relax and enjoy her time in isolation with him, free from any of the other crap that usually clung to them.

Ricco found herself falling in love with the man she was getting to know on the island. For now, she would just enjoy their time together. When it was over, she would lock her feelings away in her heart and move on with her life. That's all she could do.

He'd convinced her to stay in the main house while he continued sleeping in the guest apartment. The cottage and the Phoenix home were both stocked with food so there was no need to go into town to get anything. She'd let Mr. Jenkins know that she was fine and didn't need anything.

Kenny told her that he didn't want to risk someone finding out she was there alone. She wasn't a fool. The things happening around them scared her. She had enough sense and just enough lack of stubbornness to acquiesce to his request. Plus she enjoyed his company.

They'd developed a comfortable routine over the past two weeks. He'd done all the cooking, they'd gone on walks, and had even taken the boat out a couple of times. She'd poured over his documents, trying to glean any other information from them, but came up with nothing. She told him she was fluent in four languages and could get around with the knowledge she had in several others. He'd been amazed at her ability with calculating numbers in her head. The numbers, to her, were sometimes a curse when she couldn't turn her brain off from seeing them everywhere. Since she'd been on the island with Kenny, the numbers didn't haunt her. She was relaxed and she felt safe with him.

Still in her ratty college t-shirt and leggings that she sometimes slept in, Ricco sipped her coffee, leaned back, and listened to the water licking the sides of the boat. She loved sitting on the patio waiting for the dawn. It was still at least an hour away. She could not seem to kick the habit of getting up well before the sun. Most times she just sat in her room and read or worked on the cookbook she was creating. This morning, she couldn't seem to keep still. Her breathing was back to normal and she spoke much clearer. She just had to be careful not to overexert herself. So far, Kenny made sure that she didn't have to lift a finger. Today, it was her turn. She felt like baking something—anything. She wanted to command the kitchen again.

She hadn't dared make biscuits. She didn't want him to think this was a competition, plus she wasn't sure if her biscuits were at all better than Kenny's. For him, she'd pulled out the big guns and made her extra-large, super cheesy, extra melty, stuffed with goodness, croissant sandwiches.

She figured in the time it took to proof the dough and make the sandwiches, Kenny would be awake.

Hoping he was up by now since it was a fairly decent time for normal people to be up for breakfast, she knocked gently. She heard him shout something so she turned the knob and found it wasn't locked. Cautiously she entered and placed the food on the counter, not certain if he was in the midst of getting dressed or not. She'd eaten in the guest apartment only once since they'd been on the island. Most days they'd taken their meals on the patio, except for the few times they'd been on the boat all day. On those occasions, he packed food for them to eat while they were away.

The man surprised her at every turn. The cooking, baking, and especially his skills on the boat made her appreciate her decision to stay in the house with him. He was fascinating. He'd taught her how to drive the boat and even how to work the sails when they decided to turn off the engines in the middle of the Atlantic. They'd talked for hours about nothing in particular and everything. She'd told him about the spring time when she visited her grandmother and he'd shared stories of how he'd come to love building things with his hands—creating dreams for people.

"Frances!"

She nearly dropped the plates she'd pulled from the cabinet. It was Kenny. The emotion in which he screamed the name was far too familiar. She'd felt that kind of pain before.

Without thinking, she rushed towards the bedroom area. He was sitting up, chest bare, arms reaching for something or someone, she couldn't tell which. "Frances!" He screamed again. His tone roused the edges of her own nightmares. She quickly shook away images of her parents lying dead on the floor.

She was sure that's what this was—a nightmare. She wondered if this had anything to do with the failed mission he briefly spoke of or something else entirely. All he'd said was that he hadn't been able to save the subject.

Was Frances a love interest?

"Kenny!"

His eyes shot open. The torment in them made the hair on her arms stand on end. He was still reaching. "Kenny?" He didn't see her.

He was still asleep.

She probably should have been more concerned about waking a person in the mist of what looked and sounded like a nightmare, but she crawled onto the bed and became the thing he reached for.

"Frances!" He called out again. Grabbing her, his arms squeezing her tightly. "Frances." His voice broke on the single word and he began to cry, sitting up in bed holding on to her. She'd dreamed of being crushed by the strength in his arms, but not like this.

Definitely, not like this.

When and if the time came again, she wanted to be emotionally whole and she wanted the same for him. They had more in common than he knew.

"Shhhhh. It's OK, it's OK." She said softly trying to hide the quiver in her own voice and really wanting him to hear and believe that she would do her best to make everything OK. Her heart broke for him. Whatever was tormenting him, she wanted to make it better. "I'm here, Kenny. It's me. It's Naricco."

"I'm sorry. I'm so sorry." He sobbed, his chin resting on her shoulder. She knew he was still speaking to this Frances person.

"Wake up, Kenny. Wake up." She pleaded softly. "Please." She didn't know what else to say or do. "Wake up, baby." She whispered and crooned for several minutes before she felt him stiffen.

Several moments passed before he spoke. "Naricco?" He was awake, but she didn't let him go nor did he pull away.

Nodding, she whispered. "Yes, I'm here. I got you." He groaned next to her ear and oh how that sound did something to her. "I'm here, Kenny." Her Japanese accent lacing the words. It was always apparent when she was very emotional. "I'm here." She whispered over and over until the words were no longer a statement, but rather a confession.

They sat like that for several minutes. Ricco could feel his heartbeat against her chest—an intimacy she never thought she'd feel again. His skin was warm and damp.

Slowly he loosened his hold on her, but didn't completely let go. Ricco tilted her head to look into those eyes that always seem to be able to see into her soul where all her secrets scratched at the surface. His eyes no longer held the pain of his dream. The hurt burned away and was replaced with something else she hadn't seen in them in quite some time—desire.

Desire.

For her.

Ricco, emboldened by the need to comfort the man who'd once chased away her fears, leaned up and moved her mouth over his. He was her drug and she wanted to drown in the sensations only he could gift.

A sense of urgency and a need they could almost touch, captured them both and the kiss took on a life of its own. Of course, she'd kissed him before, but this time, this time she was certain they wouldn't stop there. And she was ready for whatever waited beyond this kiss.

"Naricco." He murmured when she reluctantly pulled away to breathe.

"Kenny." Her reply mirrored his.

No other words were spoken. They were not needed. His hands stroking the length of her back and the passionate kisses along the length of her neck spoke for him. His touches told her she was wanted. Her gentle push against his chest to shove him flat against the bed, told him that he could have her.

Kenny gently rolled them both on their sides so they were facing each other. His eyes held hers while his strong hands explored the lines of her arms and side. Every single place he touched branded her his and she was perfectly fine with that.

He pulled her closer, seizing her lips like they belonged to him and him alone. She wanted to touch him all over at once, wanted to kiss him until his heart healed, wanted to make love to him until he was all she knew.

So she did.

Chapter 17

Was this real? How had his nightmare turned into his dream of holding, touching, filling, Naricco?

He'd spent too many nights wanting this. Too many nights dreaming of making love to her. Here she was, in his space, his bed, his arms. He really didn't care if it was a dream or not. Everything about her was real to him. She'd turned his pain into passion and he never wanted to let her go, never wanted to know what it felt like to not have her at his side. The reality of his last thought no longer scared him. He was not going to let someone keep him from living his life. He was going to find out who was behind all of this and he was going to make sure to put an end to them.

Ricco was nestled against his front and he could feel himself growing hard for her again.

"I see that you're awake." She said, pressing against him.

"I see that you must want to play again."

"Is that what we were doing? Playing?"

"I don't care what we call it. I just want to do it again, to make sure you are really here. But if you aren't really here, I don't want this dream to ever end."

"So you mean to tell me that my declaration of being on birth control and having a clean bill of health in the middle of you pulling off my panties, wasn't real enough for you?"

"That was the sexiest shit I'd ever heard in my life. I thought I heard myself say that I was safe too, but all I could focus on was that we could come together, skin to skin." He snuggled against her neck. "No pun intended." He added, when he realized what he'd said. She laughed and it was the most beautiful sound. "How did you end up in my bed anyway, not that I'm complaining." He reached around and found her nipple. It bloomed under his touch, her arousal as instant as his.

Kenny didn't get an answer to his question, because the moment she rolled over and faced him, he captured her mouth and continued the process of claiming her. What was it about Naricco Maki that turned him inside out? He felt completely exposed and vulnerable with her, but the most surprising part was that he didn't care.

Morning slowly turned into afternoon and Kenny had no desire to leave the bed. He had everything he wanted wrapped in the circle of his arms and legs. However, the growl rising from beneath the covers begged to differ.

"Was that you or me?" She asked with a giggle.

"That time, I think it was you. I guess I need to feed us both." He untangled their limbs and reluctantly went to the bathroom. He again noticed the bottle of perfume and realized she must have stayed here that last time she'd visited. Again, he marveled at how their lives overlapped at certain points. He reached in to start the shower. "Care to join me?" He shouted over his shoulder.

"Absolutely."

Kenny startled at the voice so close to him. He turned and saw a naked Ricco standing in the doorway. Food no longer on his mind, he filled his eyes with her and his heart almost burst with a feeling that he thought was long lost to him.

"Since I've been feeling so well, I was going to suggest we go into Charleston, today." They'd finally drug themselves from the shower and were getting dressed.

"We still can." He replied, looking forward to exploring the historical town with her.

"Let's eat first."

"I can whip something up."

"No need. That's how I'd ended up here in the first place. I was bringing breakfast."

"Yeah?"

"Yeah." She replied, heading to the kitchen. "Let me just pop these sandwiches in the oven for a little bit and they will be good as new. Kenny watched her take a look in the fridge. "Oh good. You have salad stuff. I can make a quick salad and we can turn my breakfast sandwich into lunch."

"Sounds great. Need my help?" He asked, pulling on a t-shirt. "Do you think I need to put on a polo instead of this t-shirt, in case we decide to go grab some dinner this evening."

"Nah. Don't need any help and the t-shirt is fine. How about we grab dinner to go and eat it on the boat so we can watch the sun set."

"Sounds romantic."

She looked over her shoulder, smiled, popped a cucumber in her mouth, and kept on preparing the salad. He slid onto a stool and just watched her move with ease around the kitchen.

"I love this house." He said.

"Me too." She cooed. "You should build me one just like it." He knew she probably made the comment off hand, while busily getting their lunch together, but he was in the business of making her dreams come true.

"Ok."

When the weight of his reply reached her, he watched her pause a moment, but she didn't respond or look up at him. He grinned to himself, wondering where he'd build their house.

"Ricco! This is delicious!"

"They are my specialty."

"Does Symphony's sell these?"

"No." She laughed softly. "Why?"

"Good, because I don't want you to make these for anyone else but me."

He saw the tint creep up her face and she avoided looking at him. "OK."

Her reply thrilled him to his soul.

It was a beautiful day for an outing. The humidity was practically non-existent and the heat wasn't too oppressive even though it was nearly the end of June. A gentle breeze kept them comfortable while they walked through the markets.

"I miss the open markets of home." Kenny smiled at her and reached for her hand. "Oh my God! And the street food! I really miss that!"

"What's your favorite?"

"Everyone loves okonomiyaki, but sometimes, depending on the vendor, there's too much going on in the dish. There was a man near my school who made them perfectly."

"What's okonomiyaki?"

"It's a Japanese pancake, but not like anything you're thinking of. More like a pizza than a breakfast pancake."

"Is that your favorite?"

"I also love yakitori, chicken grilled on a skewer. But I guess my favorite is hanami dango, fresh off the grill. I used to get it when I visited my grandmother in Yoshino." Her face lit with the memory. "It was served in the spring during the time of the cherry blossoms." She looked up at him knowing he didn't know what that was either. "It is a rice dumpling sweet. There are three on a stick, green for summer grass, white for winter snow, and pink for the cherry blossoms."

"I love how everything has meaning. I assure you, there is nothing at a food truck that has such symbolism."

"Sometimes it is all nonsense, but I miss my country."

He wanted to ask her more about her home but didn't want to venture into an area that would cause her pain. So, he decided to change the subject. "Want to look at some of the baskets?"

"Sure."

He'd heard of the basket women in Charleston. How they sat right there in the market and wove the baskets they sold. The markets sold everything from baskets to cheap trinkets with your name inscribed. Ricco was looking at some beautiful wooden plaques with the meaning of a name.

"Now you know, your name won't be on any of those."

"I know. I'm looking for Cadence."

"That's pretty rare, too."

"Well, I was thinking if they had Teagan, then there may be a chance Cadence is up here too."

Kenny shook his head and walked away to look at some art pieces that caught his eyes. The market was full of everything from trinkets to fresh produce.

"Free one!" He heard Ricco exclaim. He turned and she was rushing his way. "The free one! Frances! That's the answer, Kenny."

Kenny had no idea what she was talking about. "What?" He saw her look around before she spoke again. He looked around too. "Kenny, the code. Remember?"

"The code?"

"Come on." She grabbed him by the arm and led him out of the nearest exit. She looked around again like she was making sure no one was following them. Spotting an empty bench, she led him to it. "The code from your documents repeated, 'the free one,' over and over. This morning you kept screaming the name 'Frances.'"

"And?"

"Those plaques back there had the meanings of names on them and on the one that read 'Frances,' it said the meaning is 'the free one.'"

He'd had no idea that he'd screamed her name in his sleep. Could this possibly mean that all of this had something to do with Frances?

"Come on. We need to get back to the boat." He said. For some reason, he looked around, too. All of a sudden feeling as if they were being watched. He reached for Ricco's hand, pulled her close, and headed to the nearby dock to get back on the boat where they could be completely alone from prying eyes and ears.

Chapter 18

"Thank you so much for being here, Ian." In traditional Ian fashion, he simply nodded, straightened his apron, and got back to work. Symphony smiled and headed out to speak to the counter workers. The bakery was set to open in an hour. She hated that Ricco would miss the grand opening, but preferred that she was away. She wouldn't be able to resist being at the shop.

Symphony was surprised when Ian offered to come up to Boston to give her a hand after the fire. He'd been genuinely concerned about Ricco and seemed disappointed that she was not in town. Symphony was surprised at his concern at first—it was so out of his character. Later, she realized that since Symphony's in St. Augustine had opened, years ago, Ian and Ricco had started their day together. As subtle as it was, she figured, they'd developed some sort of friendship.

"Hey baby, is there anything you need me to do?" Symphony smiled before looking over her shoulder at her husband.

"You can come over here and give me a good luck kiss."

"I'll give you a kiss, but you don't need it for luck. There's already a line down the sidewalk"

Her head shot up from the paperwork she was reviewing of the large pre-orders.

"A line?"

"Why do you sound so surprised?"

"I am!"

"Babe, Symphony's is famous. And especially after the fire, people in the area really want to show you support."

Symphony looked around at her staff busily doing their assigned tasks. She didn't like talking about the fire in front of them. She didn't want them to worry about a threat at the shop. "Let's go upstairs."

"Am I in trouble?" Kyle asked as he followed her to the office.

"Do you want to be?" She turned towards him and found him eyeing her behind. "Look Mr. Dean. We are opening in an hour, so whatever you have on your mind, you may as well get it off right now." She turned back to reach for the door. "Save it for closing time."

"Closing time? Do you plan on being here at closing time?"

"Absolutely." She placed her folder on the desk and faced him. "Kyle, it's the first day. I have to be here just in case there's a problem."

"I thought that's why Ian was here."

"Yes, but…"

"I know, Symphony." He pulled her into his arms—her antidote to whatever ailed her. "We will stay all day."

"We?"

"Yes. Well at least for as long as Cadence lasts." He lifted her chin. "Now, what did you want to talk to me about?"

"The fire."

"What about it?"

"I don't like talking about it in front of the staff."

He thought a moment as if he was trying to remember what he said. "Oh. I'm sorry."

"I just don't want them to worry about being in danger while working here."

"I get it." He cocked his head in that sexy way that she liked. "What's wrong? There's something else bothering you."

"Do you think the fire may have anything to do with all that stuff with Cadence, last year?" She was talking about the kidnapping. One of her ex-lovers plotted to kidnap her daughter and as a result had taken her and Kyle's parents too. Luckily they'd been rescued before it was too late. Someone had helped the man, but the authorities could not tie him to anyone. He was at the beginning of a very long prison sentence.

"It's possible." Kyle agreed.

"Why haven't you said anything?"

"I didn't want to worry you."

"Well I am."

"We are not going to let some asshole have us looking over our shoulders or keep us from living our lives." Her eyes slid closed as he placed a comforting kiss on her forehead. "I plan on talking to Kenny about it."

"Why Kenny?"

Before he could answer, Ian was at the door. "Symphony," Ian interrupted. "Jackson and Kim need to know how to sign into the register."

"OK, I'll be right down."

"We will table this discussion for later." She said, still wondering how Kenny fit into all of this.

"Yes, ma'am." He gave her a crisp salute and wink.

Symphony's Boston location's opening day was a huge success. It was the biggest day she'd had in Symphony's history. She was feeling pretty confident about establishing her business there. In addition, to the storefront, she was partnering with Cliques, Alex's place, to provide dessert options for the restaurant as well as their catering events. So even though this building had a much smaller seating area than the one she owned in St. Augustine, there was more staff and the kitchen was much larger to accommodate the commercial business.

"Oh my God, Symphony, this is so good. I'm pretty sure I've gained ten pounds, today."

Symphony rolled her eyes. "Oh please, Sophia, you know you burn off more calories than you could possibly consume in here, from just one dance class."

"By the way, when are we going to all go dancing at Cliques?" Candice asked all the ladies.

They were having a celebratory pastry after the shop closed. Their husbands were supposed to meet them at Symphony's when they left the office. Again, Symphony hated that Ricco was missing the opening day celebrations. She'd put in so much work to get it ready.

"How about tonight?" Alex asked.

Kyle was at the condo with Cadence. She'd gotten tired of hanging out at the shop really quickly. "We don't have a sitter for Cadence."

Just then, an older black couple appeared at the door. Symphony wondered why they knocked when the sign clearly showed, "CLOSED." Alex unlocked the door, greeted the couple warmly, and Candice made the introductions.

"Symphony, please meet my parents, William and Lillian Carwin."

They both had ready smiles and offered hugs instead of handshakes. They hugged all the other ladies as well. Alex had grown up with the couple because she and Candice were best friends as kids. Sophia knew them because Candice and Sophia were married to brothers.

Symphony was the only stranger to the couple. "It's very nice to meet you, Mr. and Mrs. Carwin. Are you here for a nice visit."

"Call me Auntie Lillian, baby. And yes, we try to come for about a month in the summer. It's not quite as hot up here as it is in Baton Rouge."

"That's great." She turned to Candice. "I know you're glad to be able to spend so much time with your parents."

Candice hugged her parents again, offered them a seat and Symphony asked if they wanted anything.

"Now, William, don't you go eating all these sweets. You know what the doctor said."

Symphony watched the man give his wife a squeeze. "I won't overdo it, dumplin'. But I've been eating celery stalks and wheatgrass smoothies, so I could eat here." He turned to Symphony. "Baby girl has been telling us how great your sweets are, so I've been in training for this day." He gave her a fatherly smile and Symphony wished she knew what it was like to have parents who were so loving to each other and others.

Her parents had been neglectful at best and drug addicts who constantly screamed at each other. She hadn't seen her father since she was four. He'd called her before she had Cadence to ask for money. He was in prison at the time. She'd seen her mother only once since she'd been given to her aunt Helen, her mom's much older sister. It was the day Griffin George proposed. He thought they would start their lives out right if she'd made amends with her mother. Symphony had no interest in marriage or her mother and had not seen or heard from her since.

"Help yourself to whatever you like. Jackson will get anything you point out." She gave him a wink, "On the house." Jackson offered to stay later so he could wait on her friends so Symphony could enjoy their company.

"My kind of girl." He said, hugging her again with a sweet kiss on her cheeks.

Symphony loved them, immediately. "You too, Auntie Lillian, help yourself to whatever you like." They went over to the pastry case and "oooed and ahhhed" over what was there.

"Symphony, my parents have agreed to watch Cadence for you, while we go out tonight."

"Oh no. I couldn't ask them to do that. They are on vacation."

Mrs. Carwin was having none of that. "Now, you kids are going to go out and celebrate." She took a bite of one of Symphony's lemon puffs. "Oh my goodness! William! You've got to try this."

Everyone gave them an indulgent smile. They all knew how good it was. It was great to see others' first reactions to Symphony's.

Just then, Kyle unlocked the door and pushed in the stroller with a giggling Cadence. She was soon scooped out of the stroller by her Godmother. Alex brought her over to meet the Carwins and also introduce the Carwins to Kyle. They fell in love with Cadence immediately.

Shortly after the arrival of Kyle, The Phoenix men showed up, including Terry. Even though Ethan's last name was Powers, he was a Phoenix by blood and they all lumped him with the rest of the men when they talked about the Phoenixes.

Everyone enjoyed pastries and other sweets even though they'd planned on dinner at Cliques later. Kyle was all for the Carwins watching Cadence. They would join them for dinner and then take Cadence back to Landon and Candice's place.

Symphony laughed at something Landon said about Terry when he was little. She remembered Terry telling her the story, but without the details Landon shared. She wiped her eyes and saw a woman peering through the window. Her heart stopped and the ready laughter was immediately gone. Symphony reached for Kyle and quickly looked around. "Cadence…where's Cadence?"

"What is it, Symphony?" Kyle asked with concern.

She saw her daughter playing with Jackson. Cadence loved the friendly college student she'd recently hired and he loved playing with her. He missed his baby sister he left behind in Maine and enjoyed when Cadence was in the shop.

"Jackson, please take Cadence upstairs to the office. I'll come get her in just a moment."

"Symphony, what is it?" Kyle asked again, watching Jackson disappear into the kitchen with Cadence.

She stood, staring stoically at the woman at the window. "It's my mother."

Chapter 19

The night out dancing was postponed for another evening. Symphony refused to let Cadence out of her sight. The sudden arrival of her mother spooked her more than she was willing to admit.

Alex ordered dinner for everyone and had it delivered at her and Joshua's home. They would celebrate there, instead. Symphony considered them all family, even Terry, and wanted to talk to them about her mother. They all knew she'd been estranged from her since she was a young girl.

After dinner, the Carwins took Cadence into the family room to play. Since Symphony had not let the woman who'd given birth to her inside the shop, no one knew what she and her mother had discussed, except Kyle, of course.

"This morning, Kyle and I briefly discussed our thoughts about the arson at Symphony's and had planned on talking to you all about it later." She looked around the table at the expectant faces of all the people who'd come when Cadence was taken. The people who she considered family. The only missing faces were those of Dixon and Gloria Phoenix and Kyle's parents. "And with the sudden appearance of my mother, I'm almost convinced that what happened at my bakery was more about me than Kenny as many of you suspected."

"What do you mean?" Landon asked her and Kyle. "Kyle?"

Symphony answered before Kyle. "As you all know, I don't have a relationship with my mother, so, I was very surprised to see her at the shop today.

"What did she want?" Terry asked the question and she could tell, Kyle, bless his heart, was doing everything he could to tolerate the man. Though he did, because he was very fond of his cousins.

Symphony briefly wondered why Terry wasn't with his girlfriend. She was glad the woman wasn't here tonight, but she'd never shown up when they all got together on other occasions. Symphony placed a calming hand on Kyle's thigh. She loved him and no one else.

"She wanted her share of Aunt Helen's property and money. Basically she wanted my inheritance. Said it was rightfully hers because she was her sister, and if she'd known she'd died, she would have gotten it."

"That makes no sense. Your aunt left a will."

"I know, Alex, but she feels entitled to it anyway."

178

"How does any of this have anything to do with the fire?" Landon asked.

Symphony was exhausted. Everything leading up to the grand opening, the day at the shop, and then having her mother show up, she just wanted to curl up in bed next to her husband, and sleep for a week. Kyle answered for her.

"We still don't know who that creep who took my family was working with.

"And you think it may have been your mother?" Landon asked what most were probably thinking.

"No, but I think someone may have sent her here. She claims she saw I was opening a new store from my website, but I don't believe her."

"Why?" Several of them asked.

"Because she may have been carrying a designer bag, but she still smelled of cheap wine and cigarettes. The stench of the streets hung on her. And she knew details about my aunt's—" She corrected herself, "I mean, my property in South Carolina."

They all seemed to sit up, but it was Joshua who spoke up. "What kind of details?"

"Symphony is afraid that she'll show up at the property." Kyle answered.

"Oh Kyle, I need to call Ricco. Now, I'm not feeling so sure about her being there"

"Being where?" Several voices inquired.

Symphony forgot she hadn't mentioned to anyone that Ricco was at her place in South Carolina so she was surprised when Terry asked the question again.

"She's recuperating on the island."

"Ricco is at your place on the island?"

"Yes, why?"

"I didn't know that."

"No one did. She didn't want anyone to know."

"I wonder if Kenny knows."

"I just said no one knew she was going. I was skeptical about letting her go alone, but at the time, thought it better than having her here. She would have shown up at the shop every day."

Kyle turned to Terry. "Where is Kenny, I've been trying to reach him for about a week."

Terry looked from Kyle to Symphony. "He didn't want anyone to know, but he's at Uncle Dixon's place."

Symphony and Kyle turned to look at each other. "I talked to Ricco, just yesterday, and she didn't mention anything about Kenny."

"Maybe she doesn't know he's there, especially if they haven't ventured far from the perimeter of the perspective homes." Terry answered.

It was Landon who voiced what most were probably thinking. "Maybe they don't want anyone else to know that they're there together."

Symphony thought about that and her last conversation with Ricco. It hadn't lasted very long and Ricco had been vague at best. Could she possibly be with Kenny, like together together? She'd gone to the island to get away from the man. What a coincidence that they were there together.

"How is it that Kenny is at Gloria and Dixon's place?" She looked at Terry.

"He needed to get away to sort out some things?"

"Sort out some things?" Kyle asked him.

"He didn't say what, just that he needed some time. I offered Uncle Dixon's place, because they'd just mentioned that their house sitter fell through, just before they left for Europe. I figured it would be a win-win for them both."

Symphony eyed Kyle. He hadn't been too keen on the idea of Ricco being alone at the cottage, but finding out that Kenny was there seemed to please him, if his slight smile was any indication.

Later that evening, after Symphony and Kyle made sure that Cadence was safely tucked in bed and asleep, they went to their own room.

It had been a long day and it didn't take Kyle long to fall fast asleep. However, Symphony laid awake thinking of the encounter with her mother.

The woman had actually leaned in as if to give her a hug, but Symphony backed away, causing her to rethink her greeting.

"What? No hug for your momma?"

"What are you doing here?" Symphony asked calmly, feeling anything but.

"I saw on your website that you had a new bakery here. I'm here visiting a friend of mine and thought I'd come take a look."

"Why?"

"I just wanted to tell you how proud I am of you."

"You should have just sent a card. Or better yet, done what you've done your whole life and pretend you don't have a daughter."

She saw her mother flinch before gathering herself. She eyed Kyle. "Who's this?"

"My husband." Symphony did not offer his name. This was not meant to be an introduction. She just wanted her mother to know that she was not alone.

Kyle slipped his arm around Symphony, pulling her close. His support meant everything. The fact that he didn't try to soften this woman's arrival by pretending all was well, was the best thing he could've ever done for her. That she had this beautiful man by her side and he would stand with her against whatever the hell all of this was, meant more than he would ever know.

"My bakery is closed." She saw her mother look through the window and take in all the people inside. "I need to get back to my special guests. Why are you really here?"

Bringing her attention away from the people in the shop, she looked back and forth from Symphony to Kyle, and pursed her lips. "I heard Helen died."

Symphony raised her chin. "And?"

"I know she had all that land near Charleston and figured I could get the deed and stuff from you." Of course she was not wondering if Symphony was alright since the only family she'd ever known was no longer living. Of course she was not worried about how her sister died or if she'd suffered at all. And of course she was not at all concerned about anyone or anything but herself.

Symphony knew Kyle's gentle squeeze was meant to calm her down before she spoke. "The deed and stuff?"

"Yeah. She was my sister. She had no husband and our other sister and family are dead."

"She had me." Symphony stated, flatly, trying with all her might to control her rage at this woman who had the audacity to think her existence entitled her to anything, let alone, Aunt Helen's money and property. Because that's all she was to society, existing. As far as Symphony knew, and her presence here now told her, this woman who gave birth to her had never contributed to anything positive in her life.

The bad decisions she'd made were etched in the hard lines around her eyes and forehead. Her cold dead eyes, and a voice cracked rough and broken from too many cigarettes and sucking on a crack pipe were all the answers Symphony needed.

She wore a cheap brown wig that didn't hide the rough edges of her own gray and black hairs reaching wildly from underneath it. She smelled of desperation. And that desperation is what Symphony was most afraid of, though she would pluck her own eyes out of her head if she showed any fear. She would not give Nadine James any kind of power over her.

Winter Lightning

"I was Aunt Helen's family. She was the mother who raised me, and I was the daughter who loved her." Symphony's tone and demeanor left no question of how she felt about the woman standing before her. "She left me everything in her will. If you go near any of my properties or come to my shop again, I will have you arrested for trespassing." Symphony turned to walk back into the shop and stopped. "I don't know who sent you, or what your real purpose is here, today, but I'll tell you this, I am no longer the little scared girl who you could smack with a hairbrush to get in line. You come after me or my family, Symphony waived towards the people in the window, and I will strike back with a force of which you have never known before. You can try me if you dare, but I do not recommend it."

She and Kyle walked in the shop and without taking her eyes from the woman staring back at her, she locked the door. Eventually, she walked away, but Symphony knew she had not seen the last of Nadine James. She hoped the woman who birthed her was prepared to cross Symphony James Dean.

*****

"I don't think this is a good idea."

"You didn't seem to think so when you came crawling to me for money a few months ago. You divorced me when I was locked up, but still seemed to think I was good enough to support you and your habits. I gave you the money so you wouldn't have to keep whoring yourself out on the condition that you would see this through."

"She was so cold." Nadine shook her head. "She's married to some white man."

"He's just some photographer. I knew his daddy when we were in school. He's a nobody."

"If something happened to her, wouldn't everything just go to him? And what about those other people? She said something about them being some special guests and she even called them her family."

"I don't know, but it's not uncommon for business owners to cater to some of their vendors. We're her family!"

"You told me she would welcome my presence in her life, because she was tired of being lonely. She doesn't seem lonely to me."

"Look here Nadine, Symphony owes us! The bitch was too good to help me out when I was in prison. We knew we were shit parents, that's why we allowed her to go to Helen. She should be thanking us." Symphony's father leaned in close to Nadine's face and spoke with barely controlled rage. "She owes us and she is going to pay! You better find a way to get that money or the deed to that property in South Carolina or dropping on your knees for a ten dollar fix will be the least of your worries."

"You must be mighty desperate yourself. She's your daughter!"

"Is she? Is she, Nadine? You got proof of that? I know you woman. You were opening your legs for anyone who could give you a fix. I was just too blinded by the beauty you used to possess to even care." The disgust on his face was plain. "But look at ya. Just a withered old crackhead."

"And what are you?"

"A former crackhead who's smart enough to know when I've had enough, but still too stupid to not end up dealing with the likes of you. Now, get me that money you owe me or the people who are after me, will be hunting your ass down too. And unfortunately crackheads don't hide well."

He walked away, leaving a very shaken Nadine behind.

Chapter 20

"I'm glad we remembered to get food before getting back aboard. The sunset was picture perfect."

Looking over his shoulder from the helm, Kenny smiled at her. "You say that every time."

"And every time I'm right."

Ricco loved watching the sunset and Kenny loved watching Ricco while she gazed at it. There was such a sense of peace that surrounded her that it made his throat tighten. He found himself always so overwhelmed with a need to protect her, though, it suddenly occurred to him that she was in fact protecting *him*.

It was Ricco who'd deciphered the code and she was also the one who may have figured out the connection. When they got back to the house, he would call to inform Cliff of what Ricco had come up with.

"Let's stay out on the water tonight." Her voice had regained its strength, but her comment was so feather-light, he studied her for a moment before answering.

"Sure. We can do that."

"It's such a gorgeous night, I don't want it to end." She looked up. "Look at all those stars. It's like there are tiny holes in the sky."

"Gorgeous indeed." His eyes never left her.

"Any particular place?"

"Just somewhere quiet."

"I can do that." He drove them out a ways from shore, dropped anchor, and sat next to her, just enjoying the night and the fact that they were the only two people in the world, as far as he was concerned.

"What do you know about that firefighter?"

"I was wondering when he would come up. What took you so long?"

"Just biding my time."

"I don't know much about him. When he visited me in the hospital, I couldn't really talk, so that limited in-depth conversations."

"Hmmm."

"You don't trust him, do you?"

"No." He was surprised that she didn't appear more surprised than she did. Actually, she looked like she was expecting his answer.

"Neither do I. His interest in me was a little strange." She frowned, "Actually, I'm a little surprised that he hasn't contacted me in the past few days."

"You've talked to him since you've been here?" He tried like hell to keep the annoyance out of his voice.

"No. I've only talked to Symphony." She cocked her head a bit and he could just about guess what she was going to say. "You sound jealous. Is that why you don't like him?"

"I don't know the man."

"Don't you?"

He studied her for several seconds before replying. "I've only spoken to him in the ER briefly and the day you were leaving the hospital."

"Speaking to him has nothing to do with knowing him."

"I'm not sure I know what you mean."

"Come on, Kenny, give me more credit than that. You called the FBI or CIA or some other federal agency, because you wanted my phone number." She held up a hand. "Don't deny it." He really couldn't. "You had no suspicions about me, so I'm almost positive that you have a complete file on John." She arched a brow and crossed her legs.

"You're right, I do."

"And?"

He wasn't sure if he should tell her what he'd found out about John. He'd spoken to Cliff just before they took the boat into Charleston. How would she feel knowing the truth?"

"Do you know his last name or where he's from?"

"I believe he told me his last name is Parker. He told me once." She replied, and thought about the second part of his question. "Wisconsin, I think. When I asked, he didn't have much to say." She frowned, "Why?"

"He's only been in Boston for about six months and had only been with the fire station for a short time before the fire at Symphony's." He couldn't tell if this information was shocking or not, but he knew she would be surprised at what he was about to tell her next.

"He is known here, by John Y. Parker or John Parks."

"Here?"

"Yes, here in the United States."

"Where's he from?"

"His real name is Ye-Jun Pak. He grew up in South Korea, with his grandfather, Woojin Pak, who was once an officer in the Chinese Army. Woojin studied in England and had fallen in love with an English woman. His parents refused to allow him to return with a foreign woman. I'm not sure where they lived, or if he ever married the English woman, but they had a daughter, Hye. Hye went to school in the states, met a man, fell in love, had a son."

"John?"

"Yes."

"I knew he had Chinese in his background. It's not that dominant, but I could see it." She frowned. "But you said he grew up in South Korea?"

"Yes. John's mother and grandmother were murdered. No one knows why or by whom. All that is known is Woojin took his grandson to South Korea."

"Why South Korea? China is huge. Seems like he could have gone back to China without having to go home."

"There was once a very large population of Chinese in Incheon, Korea. The numbers have decreased significantly over the years. Maybe he felt it was best to be completely away. Maybe it had something to do with him once being an officer. Nevertheless, Woojin raised his grandson on his own, because his family never accepted the foreign child."

"I don't understand?" She shook her head back and forth slowly. "What does this all mean?"

"I'm not sure, but Cliff and I—"

"Cliff?"

"He's a business associate of mine."

"A business associate?"

"He's been helping me try to figure out what's going on."

"You trust this man?"

"Yes, I do."

"With your life?"

"I trust him with yours, Naricco."

She stared at him for a really long time, but said nothing.

"Say something." He said, finally.

She sat up straighter. "Do you think John is involved with the fire?"

"I don't know, but there is no record of him being a firefighter before he showed up at the fire station."

Ricco looked past him out into the open waters where the moon reflected there. He wanted to pull her into his arms. To take her somewhere where he could have her all to himself. He wanted to wipe the sadness from her. He had yet to ask her to tell him the story of where her sadness stemmed, but he wanted to help her get over it, if he could. The pain made her vulnerable and too trusting—otherwise, he knew he'd never made it up to her hotel room that night. Instead, he'd made it up there and had the privilege of holding her all night.

"I don't want to talk about this anymore." She stated.

"What do you want to talk about?"

"Nothing."

"What do you want to do?" For some reason he felt nervous all of a sudden around her. Like he was a teenager on the brink of his first time.

Without saying a word, she stood. Was it desire that darkened her eyes? She kicked off her flip flops and smoothly pulled off her top.

Kenny blinked.

Was she trying to kill him?

Before he could ponder the question, she unsnapped her bra and tossed it to the side—the outline of her nipples were easily visible in the moonlight. He moved to stand, but she stayed him with a tiny foot on his knee. Kenny sat back to wait so see what she would do next—his erection growing with her every movement.

When she unsnapped her shorts, his eyes moved from what her hands were doing and focused on her face. Her features were serious and heated. He vaguely heard the metal button of her shorts clink against the deck of the boat.

How had they gotten to this point? To a place where on a whim they were comfortable enough to indulge in one another. Kenny was so wrapped into everything that was Naricco Maki.

She took a step towards him. His heart thundered in his chest in anticipation. He waited.

"Tag! You're it!" She screamed as she tapped his shoulder before she quickly stepped up on the seat and up again to dive off the back of the boat.

It took him a moment to fathom what she'd done. Kenny was more worried than startled at her diving naked into a dark ocean. Without thinking, or removing any of his clothing, he jumped in after her. Too late, he realized he didn't have a change of clothes. It was the end of June, but the water was still surprisingly cool. The distance she'd swum was startling. With easy strokes he followed her, her squeals driving him to stroke harder to catch up with her.

He figured fatigue claimed her quickly, because she slowed and allowed him to pull her into his arms—both treading water. She was out of breath and leaning on him heavily, but he treaded water easily. Kenny placed his lips on hers and softly whispered, "Tag," against her mouth, but before he could get the words "You're it," out, the quiet of the night shattered with a huge explosion that suddenly flung them apart. The Atlantic swallowed him into darkness while he fought wildly to climb his way to the surface and reached in vain for Ricco.

No! No! No! The words achingly filled his head.

This couldn't possibly be happening again. His ears rang and his chest burned from the lack of oxygen. Saltwater burned his eyes. The night stripping any hope of seeing, he knew it was useless to look for her while underneath the water. He needed to reach the surface. Where was it? He willed his body to hold on just a little bit longer. He had to make it to the surface to find Ricco.

Kenny wasn't sure if his ears rang from lack of oxygen or from the explosion, but he prayed to stay conscious long enough to break the surface. Had that been the boat? His legs ached as he kicked furiously as he reached towards the hope of taking a breath and finally—

He sucked in a balloon of oxygen with his first breath and screamed her name with the next. Ricco was nowhere to be found. He splashed around wildly.

"Ricco! Dear God! Ricco!"

Chapter 21

Besides losing her grandparents and then her parents, the worst feeling in the entire realm of emotions, had to be not having anywhere to go. No place of safety, no place to claim as your own.

When she'd stolen from her hiding place at their home, panic and adrenaline pushed her to grab a bag, throw in a few items of clothing, her hidden stash of money, and a picture of her parents. She'd rushed from her home and ran with no sense of direction or destination in mind. She could not think, all she could do was run.

When she thought her feet couldn't carry her another step, she found herself on the edge of town. Looking around, she realized she'd been there before. It was near the home of a couple her parents were well acquainted with. She walked towards where she remembered their home to be, darkness was settling in. She spotted the barn. The place looked a bit overgrown and she remembered they were away for a while with their new grandson.

Maybe she could sleep in the barn and try to figure out what to do next. She tried the door. She thought it may be locked but with a little effort she was able to pry it open. It apparently hadn't been used in some time. All it held was some gardening equipment, several dust covered sacks of pebbles and soil. Surprisingly, the little barn did not smell musty or moldy, just of soil and a faint hint of sweet tobacco. She wondered if this is where her father's friend hid his tobacco from his wife.

She didn't notice the shaking until her bag dropped from her hands. The tears fell unchecked down her face. Falling heavily onto the bags of soil, she wept silently—her pain too great to contain.

She cried the entire night. That was day one.

Seventeen days passed.

Seventeen days since her parents were murdered protecting her. Seventeen days that she'd been looking over her shoulder and on that day, far enough from her bustling town, she boarded a train that would bring her close to her grandmother's village. She needed to be in a place where she'd always felt safe and loved, though she wondered if she ever would again. She spent the ride trying to think of happier times—any other times than what she was currently living through.

Baa-baa, the name she called her grandmother, was no longer in the little village. She'd died peacefully in her sleep only a year before. The pain of losing her had not dulled, but sitting on their favorite bench in the little park that they alone seemed to know about, Baa-baa seemed so close she could feel her love protecting her.

With all the money she'd earned from tutoring her schoolmates, she could have paid for a hotel or a room, but she knew no one would rent a room to a sixteen year old girl. Though she was almost seventeen, people would still ask questions. Train stations and dark alleys sheltered her. Hiding her away from the men who'd taken her parents away. Fear seeped through her every pore as she walked and found her way from one place to the next. It shook her the moment she hid herself from the evil that she was sure was searching for her. Most nights it took more than an hour for her body to settle down and her mind to stop racing with numbers.

She counted everything. The faces she'd seen that day, the cracks, the drips from a nearby faucet one night, and she counted the seconds—all of the seconds from the moment her parents were taken from her. There were two seconds that separated the deaths of her parents. Right before the gunshots changed her world she saw her father frantically search for and grasp her mother's hand.

She was certain she would lose her mind soon. This was too much. All of this. Losing her parents so violently, being forced from her home, and finding no places she felt safe. Once, she pretended to be a worker on a catering job, just to take her mind off of things. When the caterer found out that she didn't actually work for him, he paid her anyway and asked her to stay on, because she'd done such a good job. Of course, she could not.

Sitting on the little bench she admitted to herself that she was tired and really wanted to take a real shower and get a full night's sleep, but she couldn't so she stared at the tiny little pond and watched the fish dart from one spot to another. She was so so tired. She couldn't help but drift off to sleep.

"Girl! Girl!" She heard a voice on the edges of consciousness.

Startled awake, clutching the oversized bag that held all of her possessions, she stared up into eyes that were surprisingly kind. Normally she'd come into contact with suspicious glares, no doubt mirroring the suspicion in her own.

"You have nothing to fear little Kiko." The woman said, in a voice stronger than she would have guessed.

Scanning the sun-wrinkled face, she saw no recognition in the shining dark eyes taking her in.

She wanted to bolt, but was admittedly at the end of the line. Weariness laced in a lack of will rooted her to her spot. She was tired of running, wandering, and worrying. Just plain tired.

"Who are you?"

"We will talk about all of that soon enough. But first you need a nice bath and some rest."

"How do you know me?"

"There is time for questions later, Akiko."

She couldn't move. She truly wanted to trust this woman in this place where she'd always felt safe. How did this woman know her name? She was sure she'd never seen her before.

She figured the woman realized she would not move until she had some information. "I am Nanan. Your Baa-baa spoke of you often." She looked around quickly. "Come now, we must get you someplace safe. You must forget all you know here in Japan and become someone new. They will be here soon and we must not be here when they arrive."

How did she know? Did the woman know who was after her? Did she know her parents were dead? Thinking of them again filled her with a cold emptiness. Sadness and relief ruptured her soul and

Akiko could not keep the tears from spilling. It was the first time she'd cried since that night and she wasn't sure if she would be able to stop.

"Come now little Kiko, there is much to do."

Chapter 22

Just before she was certain her lungs would burst, Ricco's fingertips broke the surface and she choked on the air fighting its way into her lungs. It was sheer instinct that pushed her body to fight for air and kick to stay afloat.

"Kaasan!" She called out. "Tou-chan!" Ricco turned around and around calling for her mother and father in her native tongue.

What was happening?

Panic swept through her, pushing her beneath the surface. She fought wildly to reach the surface again, her ears ringing. It suddenly occurred to her that she was alone and her parents were long gone.

Fragments of events flashed behind her eyes, unsure if they were recent or ancient, she couldn't make sense of what was happening. She did know that she was alone. A ball of light glowed in the distance, but she wasn't sure if she should swim towards or away from it.

Where was she?

She searched around and saw no where she could swim to or float on. It would be so easy to just slip beneath the surface again and meet her parents. She missed them so much.

What was that?

Did she hear someone?

Then suddenly she heard it again—her name. It was Kenny. She then remembered jumping off the boat and Kenny jumping in after her, but what happened after that?

"Ricco!"

"I'm here! Where are you?"

Before she could yell out again, he was there grabbing her into his arms.

"Are you hurt?"

She wasn't hurt, but what she realized at that moment was that she was naked. They were far enough away from the inlet that there was no land in sight, but not far enough to have met the ocean waters. She was scared and completely exhausted. Lingering effects from the smoke inhalation.

"I'm fine." She breathed.

"We're going to be ok." He assured her confidently.

"How?" How in the world were they going to be ok? They were alone and the boat was on fire.

"I'm pretty certain Cliff is tracking us."

"Cliff?" She clung to Kenny beginning to shiver. "Your business associate?"

Before he could answer her, they saw the lights of a boat quickly approaching.

"Get behind me and hold on to my shoulders."

"Why?"

He nodded at her state of undress and she understood. What in the world was she thinking to jump into the water like that. Fatigue still found her quickly these days.

Suddenly, she began to shake, realizing that if she hadn't have jumped, she and Kenny would more than likely be dead.

She thought about his truck. How did the boat explode?

Before she could ponder an answer to that question, the boat approached them. There were two men aboard the small craft. "Do you know them." He nodded.

"Stay behind me. Hold on to my back." He ordered with a steel edge to his voice. What the hell was wrong with him. She was the one in the middle of the ocean with no clothes on.

Well…

Maybe that was his problem.

Kenny effortlessly pulled them both onto the boat, careful to keep her shielded. Blankets were quickly offered and the men didn't react at all to have pulled up a fully clothed man and a naked woman onto their boat. Ricco stared at the two men eyeing them both, cautiously. She pulled the blanket tightly around her and slumped against Kenny who was now talking on the phone to Cliff.

"If we did that then we would cause Terry and his family to most likely spend lots of time and effort on a search...No, we better call the police, that way, whoever did this would think we think this was a random act or some type of accident...No, Cliff, I'm almost certain this was a direct hit on my life...We'll be there in about forty-eight hours."

Be where? What was Kenny talking about? Why would someone want to kill him?

Kenny clicked off the phone, handed it to one of the men who were still standing there. There was nothing distinctive about either man or the boat. They looked like they were two friends out on a fishing trip. The other man showed up again with a t-shirt and a pair of swim trunks. "The boat's not that big ma'am, but there is a small berthing area below where you can put this on. We're pretty sure the authorities are on route to the boat accident. We've already sent a message that we've found two people stranded in the water."

Ricco looked at Kenny, he nodded, so she went below and got dressed in the men's clothing that were two sizes too large and wondered what would happen when the police arrived.

Chapter 23

"But where are they now?"

"Kenny says they're someplace safe."
"Why didn't they just come back to Boston? What the hell is going on? What has he gotten Ricco involved in? Wait, do you think this has anything to do with Nadine showing up? Oh my God, Kyle, what if this is all my fault? I knew I should have told her to come back after Nadine showed up at the shop."

"Symphony, we have got to trust that Kenny knows what he's doing. The police do not suspect sabotage."

"How do they know? The boat pieces are spread all over the damn inlet!" Symphony paced the floor in front of the massive window where she usually stood to admire the night lights of the city. Stopping, she turned to face Kyle. "What if they'd been on the boat?" She began to cry. Something she didn't do often. Kyle reached for her, but stilled when she blurted, "What the fuck is going on? Ricco said she wanted to go to the island to get away from Kenny.

How did they manage to be swimming so far away from land...TOGETHER?"

"Thank goodness they were." Kyle countered as he gently rubbed her shoulders.

"This shit isn't normal." She looked up at him, completely perplexed. "It's just not. This is some movie shit. I'm a freaking baker. I shouldn't have these kinds of events going on in my life. Who has these types of stories to tell?"

"We do?" He pulled her close and whispered, "Imagine the boring lives other people must have."

"You're such an idiot."

"But I'm your idiot."

"That you are."

"Come on, we're going to be late."

"Late for what?" Symphony looked up at him. She was dead tired and had no desire to be anywhere but home.

Kyle kissed her forehead. "Don't you remember? We're supposed to have dinner at Landon and Candice's. They are having a special dinner because they missed her parent's anniversary a few weeks ago." Symphony groaned. "You even offered to provide the desserts." She beat her head on his shoulder.

"That's right. Ian took care of all the details." She sighed heavily, "I guess I'll get dressed. They've been so kind to us and Cadence. I can't miss it."

"You sure?"

"Yeah." She reached up and placed a quick kiss on his lips. "I just need about twenty minutes." Symphony hurried off to the bathroom. "What time are your parents arriving tomorrow?"

"They're leaving before the sun comes up, so they'll be here around 8:00am, I believe."

"You believe?" She called out from the closet. "Isn't that something we need to know so we can pick them up?"

"They don't want us to pick them up. They insisted on taking an Uber for the first time."

Symphony stepped back into their bedroom and laid an outfit on the bed. She let out a surprised chuckle, "An Uber? Whose idea was that?"

"My dad's."

"What? Seems more like an idea Pixie would have."

Pixie is what everyone called Kyle's mom. She was more of a Pixie than a Margaret.

"I think it's his way of showing her that he's still hip."

Winter Lightning

Kyle's parents were coming to check out the new bakery and to sightsee for a couple of days before bringing Cadence to Virginia to visit some of their dearest friends who'd recently moved there.

"I'm going to jump in the shower right quick. Text Landon and tell him we'll be there in thirty minutes. That just puts us ten minutes late."

"I'll tell him we'll be there in about an hour. We can always use the baby as an excuse."

"We don't need an hour, Kyle. I'll be quick."

"Yeah, but I can't guarantee that I will."

She eyed him as he began removing his clothes. "Come on, Kyle, we need to go."

"Oh, I'm coming."

She tried to run back to the bathroom but he caught her and as always, he was her undoing.

Symphony's cell phone rang and she groaned against her husband's kiss. She wanted to ignore it, but it could be Ricco. "Raincheck?" She whined.

With a wink, he replied, "Always."

She ran back to the bedroom and scrambled to grab her phone from her purse on the bed. She didn't even look at the caller ID, she was so distracted by her handsome husband. His blond hair was starting to grow back a little floppy like she liked it. She loved that beach bum look on him. He wore it so well.

"Hello." She said into the phone while blowing a kiss to her husband.

"We need to talk."

Symphony frowned. "Who is this?"

"It's a shame you don't even know your own mother's voice.'

"What do you want and how did you get this number?"

"It ain't hard to get a cell phone number."

"What do you want?"

"I said we need to talk."

Symphony's stomach churned just hearing the woman's voice. That same voice had berated and belittled her every day until she'd been blessed to be taken away and given to her aunt Helen. "We have nothing to talk about." Symphony was about to click off the line.

"Please don't hang up, please, I need the money."

She rolled her eyes. The woman hadn't changed. It was never about having a relationship with her daughter, it was always and would always be about what she could get from her. "I'm not giving you a dime of Aunt Helen's money and I would rather burn in hell than give you a penny of what my husband and I have worked so hard to get."

"He's going to hurt me real bad if I don't get it, Symphony, please." She was crying, a ploy she always used to get what she wanted. Even at the age of four, Symphony remembered her mother crying to try to get a few more days to pay the rent. Crying when she claimed she'd lost her wallet when she was trying to get a pack of meat to feed her poor little hungry child.

Symphony had news for Nadine Dean: those tears meant nothing to her. Symphony had cried too many of her own at her mother expense to care even a little.

"You don't know what he's capable of. He says you owe us."

"Who is 'us?'"

"Your father. I'm afraid of what he may do. He wants fifty thousand dollars or that property."

"Well he's not getting either. I'm not afraid of him or you! I'm no longer a little girl to be pushed around and treated like trash, so you and him can both just go to hell and take your threats there with you!"

Symphony was shaking when she threw the phone on the bed.

Dinner was being served when they arrived at the party. Not in the mood for a party, but she refused to let her parents put a damper on even a second of her day.

The entire gang was there—all the Phoenix brothers and their wives, and Terry was there with Ava. There was something about that woman that Symphony couldn't put her hand on. She was just too…too nice and incredibly doting on Terry. It was like she was trying so hard to show everyone that she was a great girlfriend. She constantly bragged on him and went on and on about the future they were going to have.

It was quite awkward. Not because Symphony was his ex-girlfriend, but because it was annoying to everyone. Even Terry seemed irritated most of the time.

Symphony was actually surprised to see her with him. He hadn't brought her to any recent functions. This was the first time Symphony saw the woman since before her shop opened.

Alex caught Symphony's eyes at dinner and gave a slight eye roll. She didn't like Terry's girlfriend at all. Alex thought the woman too clingy and too much in the guys' business. She never wanted to gather with the ladies, just always mixed up with the men. Everyone could tell it annoyed Terry, which is probably why she wasn't invited to too many gatherings. Who knows. Maybe she went to lots of places with Terry and Symphony just wasn't there.

Dinner was delicious. Candice told everyone how she had to keep kicking her mom out of the kitchen while the catering company prepared the finishing touches of the meal.

After dinner, Symphony cornered Terry, Landon, and Ethan to try to get some information about the boat explosion and where Ricco and Kenny were now. The only thing she learned was that Dixon hired a team of experts to look into the matter and to do a sweep of the island to make sure nothing was amiss.

"They aren't cutting their trip short are they?"

"No, they figured there was nothing they could do and felt it was safer to be away while the authorities and his private investigators found out what was going on." Landon answered.

Ethan added, "I'm sure Kenny and Ricco are safe." Ethan reached for the baby. Cadence went to him willingly. Symphony saw him look over at his wife and they both shared a tender smile. Symphony knew the couple couldn't conceive their own child, but had adopted a little girl they adored.

Kyle watched his wife as she talked to Terry, Landon, and Ethan. He saw how Ethan's face lit up while holding Cadence. He also saw Ava sitting off alone and watching them. The look of malevolence she targeted at Symphony as Symphony waved bye-bye to Cadence and walked away from the men startled him. Ava caught Kyle's eyes and her face transformed to a smile and pleasant features so quickly that he questioned whether he'd really seen the malice on her face. However, he was certain he had not imagined it.

Symphony took a moment to look at Landon and Candice's wedding pictures, displayed so creatively on one of the family room walls. She guessed that was to be expected since Candice was an artist and ran an art gallery. She glanced over to see Cadence still playing with Ethan and the other guys. She was surprised Ava wasn't there loitering. Turning back to one of the portraits, she wondered briefly where they'd taken it.

"You know he doesn't love you anymore."

What the f—

Symphony heard the familiar voice behind her, raised an eyebrow, and slowly turned towards it. Speak of the devil and it shall appear, she thought. Ava Fletcher stood there sweeping her hair to the front of her shoulder. She wore a bright smile that was as fake as the hair she fussed with constantly.

"I beg your pardon?" Symphony asked, coolly.

"Terry. I know you love him."

"Of course I do, I consider him a dear friend, but if you're suggesting that I have romantic feelings for him, you couldn't be further from the truth." Symphony watched something wicked cross Ava's features. Her eyes narrowed as Symphony continued, "I'm in love with my *husband*. So you have nothing to worry about."

"Oh, sweetie, I'm not worried. Terry is totally committed to me."

It took everything Symphony had not to cuss her up one side and down the other, but she was trying to clean up her foul tongue since she'd become a mother. Instead, she said, "Well, if you thought that, you wouldn't be all up in my face. It's truly a sad look for you and this entire scene stinks of pettiness." Symphony didn't miss her stiffening and how her jaw tightened. "Now, if you'll excuse me." Symphony brushed past her, feeling the hatred from the pretentious cow burning her back.

"What was that about?" Alex asked Symphony as Symphony joined her at a collage of paintings she was sure Candice painted. "I just saw Ava storm out of here."

"Oh just some girl talk."

"Girl talk, huh?"

"Yep."

"It looks like Ava just—"

"How did you like the cake, Alex?"

"Delicious as usual." Alex replied eyeing her friend, but getting the message that she didn't want to discuss Ava Fletcher.

Great. Ian did all the desserts this time. He'll be out baking me soon."

"Not a chance. Anyway, they're your recipes."

"True."

"Have you heard from Ricco?"

"No," Symphony answered, "and I'm very concerned about her."

"Isn't it something how she and Kenny ended up on the island together?"

"Yes, that's one of the things I'm worried about."

"What do you mean?" Alex asked, gesturing for them to take a seat. Candice and Sophia walked in. They sat too.

"How's Ricco?" Sophia asked Symphony.

"That's what we were just talking about." Alex replied.

Before Symphony could respond to anyone, Terry and Ava walked over to them.

"You aren't leaving are you?" Candice asked. The other ladies did their best to school their faces. No one liked Ava and they were hoping she was leaving early.

Terry spoke while Ava smiled politely and hung on to his arm. "Ava isn't feeling well. I'm going to drop her off so she can take something and lie down. I'll be right back."

Startled, Ava jerked her head up, "You're not going to stay with me? You know how I get when I get one of these headaches."

"Unfortunately, I can't stay. My cousins need me to help them with something." Ava glared at Symphony like somehow it was her fault.

Symphony didn't flinch, instead she said, "It was so good seeing you again, Ava. We've been missing you. I hope you feel better soon."

"Be careful and see you in a bit, Terry." Candice offered as the couple retreated to the door. She turned to Symphony, "You should be ashamed of yourself for poking the bear."

"That's no bear, more like a dog." Symphony replied.

"A female one." Alex added.

They all burst into laughter. Something Symphony sorely needed. She was truly worried about her friend. She was sure they weren't still on the island. Mr. Jenkins called and told her that Ricco let him know that she was leaving the house.

Where in the world were Kenny and Ricco.

Chapter 24

"Where in the world are we, Kenny Cavanaugh?"

"Somewhere safe."

"So you're not going to tell me where we are?" Ricco threw down the new duffle bag full of newly purchased clothes. "Who's house is this?"

"Mine."

Ricco looked up at him. "Based on the length of time we spent on the plane, I take it we aren't in South Carolina nor anywhere near Massachusetts anymore."

"You're correct." He sat on the sofa in what she figured was the living room.

"Kenny Cavanaugh if you don't start stringing more than two words together I'm going to throttle you!" He cocked an eye at her. "I'm starting to feel like a hostage."

That was the last thing Kenny wanted. He wanted Ricco to feel safe with him. To trust him. He knew of only one way to do that.

"We're in Washington state. I built this house for Evelyn. It was where we were going to raise our family." Ricco sat on the sofa crossed legged next to him. He could tell she was wondering why he'd brought her to a house belonging to a woman he was going to marry.

"You never married." It was a statement.

"We never married."

"Why?"

"She was murdered."

He saw pain cross her features. "My parents were murdered." She offered quietly. He knew she'd encountered deep pain in her life, but never asked. He wanted her to tell him when she was ready. "Right in front of me." Tears ran freely down her beautiful features. He wanted to reach for her, but didn't want to disturb the moment. "I was hiding in the oshire." She looked up at him. It's like a closet. My father forbade me from coming out until the men were gone, no matter what happened."

She paused for so long that he was sure she would not continue. "I was alone and frightened for so many days. I had no family—nowhere to go. What happened to Evelyn?"

The question was so abrupt it took Kenny a few moments before he realized she'd asked one.

"I didn't keep her safe."

"You make it sound like it was your fault."

"It was."

"I can't believe that."

"My past is haunting me. That's why I couldn't be with you, Naricco."

"What do you mean?"

"Frances. I didn't keep her safe. She was killed, because I didn't keep her safe."

"That's the name you screamed out in your sleep. Who is Frances? Were you in love with her too?"

Kenny frowned. Is that what she thought—that Frances was a love interest? "No. Do you remember when I told you I was in the business of liberating people from dangerous situations?"

"Hai."

Kenny smiled inwardly, knowing she had no idea she'd said the word in her native tongue.

"I was liberating Frances from a dangerous situation. Her father was a high profile political figure with radical ideas. His daughter, Frances was kidnapped. I was able to remove her from the hostages, but there was a civil war in the midst of the extraction zone. I had to leave her for a moment while I put my team in place to make sure our exit strategy was still viable. There was an abandoned building." Kenny squeezed his eyes shut, not wanting to relive the moments, but knew he had to. "I was only gone a few seconds."

"What happened?" She asked quietly.

"I'm not certain, but the building exploded. The blast threw me through the glass of another building. I got up, ran towards where I'd left her and another blast knocked me off my feet again. I don't remember what happened after that. My team found me. I woke up in a hospital in Italy. They didn't find Frances. She was only six years old."

"What happened after that?"

"I was done with the business, went back home, met Evelyn, fell in love, and asked her to marry me."

"Washington is your home?"

"Yes."

"One morning we were walking in the park and a sniper shot her in the head. She lived for almost a day."

"But you said it was your fault."

"I failed my mission. Frances's father vowed I would suffer just as he suffered."

"But…"

"Ricco, someone tried to execute her in broad daylight in a family park. No one saw anything. No evidence was found. I've done things for this country that no one should have to imagine. I know a sniper shot when I see one."

He waited for the look of revulsion to appear on her features but she only looked determined.

"That was not your fault Kenny."

"I should have known what was coming. I'd become too complacent."

She placed her hand on his knee. "It was not your fault Kenny." He wanted so badly to believe her.

"When I moved to Boston and started my construction company, one thing after another kept happening. I thought that too, was part of my suffering from Frances's father. It turned out to be sabotage from a rival company."

"How do you know that Evelyn's death wasn't by some random lunatic."

"But why her?"

"Why anyone, Kenny?" She held his eyes until he had to look away.

"But what about those attempts on my life? The device found in my truck outside of your place and the boat? The coded letter."

"I think that was more about me than you."

"That's what I mean. They are after you because they think hurting you will hurt me." He stood up abruptly. He should never have gotten her involved in any of this. "And it will, Naricco." He turned towards her, defeat etching his features. "I fell in love with you the moment I saw you, and I can't seem to undo it." He walked over, dropped to his knees and placed his head in her lap. "I can't undo it…I can't undo it." He felt her slender fingers in his hair. He grabbed her hips and held her tightly. "I love you Naricco Maki."

"I am Akiko Ishida. I did not know it at the time, but my parents were killed because of me. And also, because of me, your life has been in danger. Ye-Jun Pak, the man we know as John the fireman, was most likely sent here to either kidnap me or kill me. I'm sure it's the latter."

Kenny's heart began to race and his head buzzed. It took him a moment to move. What was she saying? He sat back and stared up at her.

"Your name isn't Naricco Maki?"

How could his team not have known that?

"No, Kenny, it is not."

Chapter 25

"Terry looked upset when he came back to the party." Symphony commented as she and Kyle were getting ready for bed.

"I think he was more irritated than upset."

"Why so?"

"I heard him tell Landon that he broke up with Ava when he took her home."

"Really?"

"Yeah, from the bits and pieces I heard, she did not take it well."

"I bet she didn't. There's something wrong with that woman. You know she accused me of being in love with Terry, tonight." Symphony picked up some of Cadence's toys. "Crazy bitch!"

"Yeah, I saw her throwing some dirty looks at you, tonight."

"I basically told her that I had a whole husband and to get her petty ass out of my face. I don't think she was very happy that Terry was coming back to the party without her." Symphony squinted thoughtfully, "and it probably didn't help that I insinuated that Terry has been hanging out without her."

"I'm pretty sure that unhinged her pretty good." Kyle grabbed a bag from the closet so Symphony could put Cadence's toys inside for her trip. "I'm going to jump in the shower, then I'm going to give you your whole husband perks!" She giggled and tossed a stuffed duckie at him.

Symphony walked down the hallway to double check the guest room. Her in-laws were arriving in the morning and she wanted to make sure everything was prepared. Afterwards she headed to check on Cadence. Sometimes she woke up right before they got in the bed, but the baby was sound asleep tonight, no doubt worn out from the evening. Everyone loved her and wanted to play with her.

The doorbell rang. Symphony wondered if her in-laws decided to arrive early. She walked downstairs, looked around to make sure everything was all picked up, and headed to the front door.

Symphony looked through the peephole and looked again.

What the fuck!

What was she doing here?

Irritation and anger fueling her, Symphony swung the door open wide, but before she could question the woman as to why she was at her door and how she knew where she lived, there was a loud blast.

228

The sound echoed in her ears and somewhere in the distance she heard a baby cry.

Was that her baby?

Symphony looked down at her blood-soaked camisole, confused. She looked up and tried to scream, but before she could do anything else she crumpled to the floor.

"Symphony! Did you hear that? Symphony!"

Kyle quickly rinsed off, grabbed his towel and rushed into their bedroom. He heard Cadence crying from her bedroom. The noise must've woken her. "Symphony, what was that!" There was no reply.

His heart began to race.

Something was wrong.

Symphony never let Cadence cry for long. He grabbed his robe from behind the bathroom door and rushed out of the bedroom.

Kyle stopped in Cadence's room, picked the baby up, made sure she was ok, and she quieted immediately. He sat her in her crib with her favorite toy and rushed downstairs. He heard sirens in the distance before he saw her.

"Symphony!"

Her name ripped from the depths of his soul. Rushing to get to her, Kyle stumbled over the last few steps and fell onto the family room floor. Nearly blinded by his fear and tears, he lifted his head and saw his wife, the love of his life, the mother of his daughter. Kyle saw his song. The symphony to his soul. His future. His reason.

He saw his Symphony lying in a pool of blood.

He scrambled to his knees and forced himself to stand, but his feet would not let him confirm, what his heart feared. Kyle stood there for what seemed like hours. He heard Cadence cry again and all he could think was what if she got up in the morning and had no mother. This couldn't possibly be their story.

Finally with his feet and brain working together, Kyle raced to the doorway. His scream punctured the night's sky. It was raw, heartbreaking, and primitive.

What could he do? How could he save her? There was so much blood.

Who did this!

Frantically, he looked around for something, anything to stop the blood pumping from her abdomen. He spotted a pink blanket in the basket by the door. He grabbed it and placed it over what could have only been a gunshot wound. He had to stop the blood.

He had to save his wife.

After only a few seconds the blanket was soaked in blood. He'd been here before, done this same thing. It was what happened during war. But this wasn't war. This was his home, his life. This was his wife lying beneath him and he was at a complete loss.

Kyle didn't notice the red and blue lights reflecting off his family room walls. He didn't comprehend when the first responder asked him what happened. He only knew two things.

"She's my wife. There's so much blood. She's my wife...she's my wife..." It became a mantra.

"Sir, what happened?"

Kyle stared up at the man who'd shoved him out of the way and fought like hell to comprehend what was going on. Somehow he managed to say, "I was in the shower. I heard a loud bang. It sounded like a gunshot."

Cadence wailed upstairs. Kyle's gaze turned towards the stairs. "My daughter." He looked down at Symphony. "This is her mother."

Time moved in slow motion, but in reality the paramedics were moving at lightning speed carefully placing Symphony onto a board and putting her on the gurney. Everyone seemed to all talk at once, but all he could see was the blood-soaked baby blanket in his blood-covered hands.

His wife's blood. Somewhere in the fog he heard, "There's a faint pulse!"

"Sir we need to take her, we're going to need some information. Is there someone we can call for the baby."

"My parents coming in morning." He mumbled.

"Sir!"

Kyle looked up at the man.

"He's in shock." Someone commented.

"Oh my God! What happened?" Kyle looked up into Ian's face but did not seem to recognize the man."

"Mr. Dean! What happened!"

"She's my wife…there's so much blood…"

"Sir, who are you?" The police officer asked Ian.

"I'm Ian Palsar. I work for the Dean's at the bakery down the street. I'm staying in a condo right near here. I was walking home when I saw the lights"

"Do you know if there's anyone we can call? He says there's a baby upstairs and he isn't in any condition to look after the baby right now.

"Yes, the Phoenixes. Alex and Joshua Phoenix are the Godparents. I'll call them."

"We're going to need someone to come to the hospital as quickly as possible."

"If someone stays here with Mr. Dean, I can go in the ambulance." Ian said to one of the officers. Kyle was in no shape to be of any assistance right now.

They rushed Ian to the ambulance. There was no time to waste.

The area was swarming with police. Neighbors were coming out of their homes and being questioned. Kyle was oblivious to it all.

"She's my wife…there's so much blood."

Chapter 26

"I changed my name when I fled Japan. Nanan was with me for a little while. I don't think she ever returned. I think she has family in New York, but I'm not certain where she went once I was registered for college. Let me tell you the story."

Kenny stood from his position on the floor and sat next to her. She told him of the days right after the death of her parents—the loneliness and fear. She told him about meeting Nanan at the pond.

"By that time, I was tired of being afraid and tired of wandering and worrying. When she spoke of Baa-baa," she saw the confusion on his face and explained. "Baa-baa is what I called my grandmother."

"How did you get there?"

"I took a risk and rode the train, but by then I'd made my way far enough away from my home that no one would be looking for me in that train station. At least that's what I hoped." She continued her story.

"The woman obviously knew who I was, even though I didn't remember ever seeing her and when she spoke of my grandmother, all I could do was cry." Even now her throat tightened just thinking about how relieved she was to finally be able to rest.

234

"I went with Nanan to her small home and it reminded me so much of Baa-baa's that I couldn't stop crying." Kenny wiped away a tear and she leaned into his warm hand and smiled at him. She was sure he would be angry when she revealed that he was probably in danger because of her, but he didn't know it all yet.

"Nanan fed me, I bathed and she insisted I rest." Ricco gave a small chuckle. "I rested for nearly two whole days."

"I imagine you were exhausted. That's usually how I slept when I returned from a mission."

"When she figured I'd rested enough, she sat me down and told me the truth about my parents. My grandmother had confided in her in case I ever needed help. Nanan was connected to some very powerful people and she and my grandmother had been friends since they were girls."

"Why would she think you would ever need help?"

"Because she knew of my gift and how valuable it would be in the wrong hands. Baa-Baa had it too, though I never knew that."

"What gift?"

"Numbers."

"Numbers?"

"Yes."

"Like the code you were able to break?"

"Yes, but I see numbers differently. Sometimes they appear in my mind in different colors. Kind of like synesthesia, but more than that. I can read numbers like most people read words. They always tell a story." He frowned and tilted his head. "I don't call it a gift. I call it a curse. Especially when I'm anxious, worried, or stressed." She stretched out her legs and stood. She walked to the window and looked out at all the green covered mountains in the distance. "Like that night you came up to my hotel room. You were such a relief, because I couldn't stop counting."

"Counting what?"

"Anything. The seconds, minutes, hours. The seconds in the hours, the seconds in the minutes, and the seconds between the noises in the hotel. And I can add up anything. I see numbers everywhere. They are always popping in and rolling all around in my head. Sometimes the colors give me a headache. I try hard to control it with meditation and other tricks I've learned over the years."

She walked back over and sat next to Kenny. "My parents both worked for a software company developing computer software. We weren't poor like many families in our city, but we were nowhere near rich. So while others at their job would brag about owning their own home and taking trips, my parents bragged about me. They spoke of me often and my talent for math.

"Soon, they began coming home with software designed as brainteasers. It was a game to me. The tougher they were, the better. There was no code I couldn't crack, no puzzle I couldn't solve. I found out from Nanan that my parents were unknowingly working for a company that was gathering intelligence on China. They didn't know at first, but both were very intelligent people. Somehow, my father detected a ghost in one of the programs, which was a backdoor that revealed a decoder for an underlying program." She waved her hands seeing his brows bunch. "It's all really complicated, but the gist of it all was my parents were smart enough to figure out the seemingly benign, already complicated programs they were coding, were embedded with a microcode with encrypted intelligence.

"My father thought it was a flaw in the software and brought it to management's attention, still not knowing he was encrypting some sort of spyware. Management assured him they would take care of it and to basically do his job and create the software they needed for their customers. Suspicious, my father copied one of the programs and brought it home. I found it and put it in my computer thinking it was another game. It was a really tough one. Of course, I didn't recognize the message, but I knew it was some sort of message. Unfortunately, we live in a world where nothing is secret. They traced the software back to my computer and a few hours later, two men were holding guns to the heads of my parents. Basically, they wanted me in return for their lives. I could do something their computers couldn't. My parents insisted they didn't know where I was and were killed."

The pain was still so fresh, but no tears fell. "So, after Nanan found me, I left with an inheritance I never knew my grandmother left me and a new identity. Now, I am sure I have been found out."

"How do you figure the fireman fits into all of this?"

"I don't know. I was hoping you could help me find out who's at the root of all of this so I can go on with my life."

"How do you envision that life?"

She wanted desperately to say, "with you," but she wasn't sure how he felt about her now that she'd revealed who and what she was. "I love the life I've created since I've been in this country. It's simple and

I get to do what I love." She chuckled sadly, "Well it was simple until all of this."

"What did you want to grow up to be when you were a girl?" He asked her.

"I wanted what all Japanese girls are supposed to want."

"And what's that?"

"A kind Japanese husband, a fine house, and sons to carry on his name."

"I can help you out with most of that?"

She stared at him and then looked around the room. "Kenny Cavanaugh, I am not living in a house you built for another woman." It was a beautiful home, but she knew that every beam, fixture, room, and furnishing would remind him of her. Ricco had no desire to live with a ghost.

"You've already told me what kind of house you want."

"I did?"

"Yes. You told me that you wanted a house on the water just like Dixon and Gloria's"

"Did I?" She smiled. "And what about a kind Japanese husband?" She began to tremble.

Kenny sat back, reached out for her and she came willingly. He pulled her onto his lap. "I bet if we did a DNA ancestry kit, it'll show a hint of Japanese on there somewhere and I know how to use chopsticks."

Kenny made her feel alive. He took the sadness away and allowed her to feel her whole self without the demons. She loved Kenny Cavanaugh and wanted to provide him with all the sons and daughters he wanted to have.

"And I can use a fork."

"I can't guarantee sons, but I sure can guarantee lots of practice."

She wanted him to kiss her. She wanted to know that they could be together—that he wouldn't offer her safety and love then decide to leave her.

"I won't do that again." She looked up at him. "I can see the doubt taking over your brain."

She rolled her eyes. "Stop acting like you know me."

"I love you, Naricco, or Akiko. I don't care what your first name is, but I'd like to change your last name to Cavanaugh."

"Let's get through this mess and we'll see."

"You will be mine. This mess will be over soon and that's all to it."

"OK."

She desperately wanted to believe him.

At the moment, Ricco didn't care who he'd built the house for. She wanted Kenny Cavanaugh—right here, right now. Still on his lap, she turned to straddle him. Taking his head in her hands, she wanted him to feel how much she loved him, even though she could not say the words yet.

Kenny's phone rang. "Leave it," she said against his mouth.

"I can't. It's Cliff."

Ricco sat back while he reached for the phone in his pocket. "What's up, Cliff?" There was a pause. Kenny looked up at her. "We're on our way."

Ricco frowned. Where were they going now? They'd only just arrived in Washington. He clicked off the phone.

Something was wrong. She could see it in the seriousness of his eyes and the set of his jaw. "What?" She heard herself say. "There wasn't another fire, was there?"

"No. Symphony has been shot. They aren't expecting her to make it."

Chapter 27

Kenny saw Cliff immediately when they exited the secure area of the terminal in Boston.

"I don't think it's safe for you to be back here."

"We know, but Ricco insisted on being here."

Kenny could tell his friend gave pause to his mentioning of "we."

"There's been a development." Cliff stated flatly and Kenny knew that was Cliff's way of telling him that they needed to speak in private.

"What's happened? Will Symphony be OK?" Ricco asked Cliff.

The anguish in Ricco's features was plain to see. Her eyes were red and puffy. She'd cried the entire flight, convinced that somehow this was all her fault. Guilt was eating her alive and each tear that fell scraped at Kenny's insides. It literally pained him to see her in pain.

Cliff turned to look at Ricco and extended a hand. With everything going on and with both of them knowing so much about the other, Kenny had forgotten the two hadn't actually met. There was so much to catch him up on.

"My apologies." Kenny interjected.

"Ricco, this is my good friend Cliff Richards. Cliff, Narrico Maki." Kenny didn't miss the hint of suspicion in Cliff's gaze.

He knew that look.

Cliff didn't trust Ricco.

The two shook hands

"I've heard a lot about you Ms. Maki. Glad to finally meet you in person." He sounded friendly enough, but Kenny knew better.

"How's that possible? Kenny barely knew me before this morning and I know he hasn't spoken to you at all today?"

Cliff looked from Ricco to Kenny and back to Ricco. She held his gaze. Kenny did his best to school his face, but he knew his friend was not expecting that comeback. Oh how he loved the fire that lived inside of her. All this time he felt he needed to shield her, to be the strength she needed, but it was she who gave him strength. It was she who made him feel whole again.

Kenny placed his hand at the small of Ricco's back to urge her forward. "How about we save our conversation for the ride to the hospital." He could tell by Cliff's demeanor that he didn't think going to the hospital was a good idea at all.

A gray SUV pulled up and they all climbed inside.

"So Cliff's got you driving him around now, Ted?" Kenny said to the driver of the car. He hadn't seen his former teammate in quite some time. Not since some of their first missions. Cliff was calling in the big guns.

"I told him he sure as hell better not get used to this shit, because it won't happen often." Ted seemed to notice Ricco for the first time. "Sorry ma'am, I don't normally talk like that in the presence of a lady. She waved him off.

"How do you all know each other?" Ricco asked.

"Old business associates." Cliff stated coolly— too coolly for Kenny's liking.

"Now, what's this new development? It must be mighty important for you to call in Ted here." Ted's eyes sparkled with laughter as he eyed Kenny from the rear view mirror.

Cliff looked over his shoulder from the front passenger seat. "Maybe we should speak in private." He gritted.

Ricco looked at the two men and was about to say something, but Kenny stopped her with a soft hand on her thigh. "I assure you Cliff, that you can speak freely.

Cliff didn't look convinced. "It can wait."

"You know my true identity, don't you Mr. Richards?" She threw up a hand. "Never mind, you don't have to answer that. If you are as good as I assume you are, then you must know."

She straightened in her seat and Kenny almost felt sorry for Cliff. "I assume you're some sort of private detective, civilian SEAL, or what Kenny calls a liberator. You know…the type of guy you always want on your side. Well, if that's who you are, there is no way, even with the connections my grandmother and Nanan may have had with who knows who, you surely know who I am."

Kenny could see the grin on Ted's face.

"Well?" She added. "Do you?"

"Yes, Akiko, I know who and what you are."

Kenny frowned, but didn't interrupt. Naricco did not need his help.

"And what do you think I am?"

"Like you said, I am that good, so I don't think it, I know what you are."

"And that is?"

"A spy for the Chinese."

"You do know I'm Japanese, right?"

245

Kenny had had enough. "She is not a Chinese spy, Cliff, though I know how you would get that impression." He turned to Ricco, "I know this is not the time or the place and you're upset about your friend, but will you please tell him your story."

So she did.

And after the telling, Cliff seemed satisfied.

"I'm sorry to have to put you through that Ricco, but I had to be sure.

Kenny knew Cliff to be a human lie detector. He was testing her. He wanted to punch his friend for making her relive the worst part of her life, but he knew Cliff was only looking out for him.

"I'd like to stop by my condo before we go to the hospital. Is that possible?" Ricco asked no one in particular, though Ted responded that it would be no problem.

When they arrived at her place, the door was cracked a bit. Kenny looked up and down the sidewalk, then at the two men in the car.

"No need to panic, Ian's been staying here since I've been gone." Kenny held up a hand suggesting they were fine for a moment, but there was still a sense of unease creeping up his spine.

"Maybe he forgot to close it all the way."

In a hushed tone, Kenny directed her back to the car. "Why don't you go wait in the car while we check out the place."

"Don't be absurd. You'll scare the man to death if the three of you rush in there like the SWAT team." By this time, Cliff and Ted were out of the car. She rolled her eyes and stepped into the foyer. "It won't take but a second," she called out over her shoulder.

Kenny quickly scanned the living room and noticed a piece of mail on the floor, when he reached to retrieve it, he spotted a tap at the edge of the counter. Senses on high alert, he began to notice other things. Items that had been moved. The dust on the shelves showed they weren't placed exactly back where they'd been before. Yes, Ian could have done that, but his gut told him someone had rifled through her home.

"Ricco!"

When there was no answer he rushed towards what he assumed was her bedroom. There she was. Wide-eyed and furious, a gun being held on her by the fireman.

He pushed away the flash of Evelyn being shot in the head at his side. He would not let that happen. The only way out of the condo was through a window or the front door. Either way, the man would not be able to get past Ted and Cliff.

"There's no way out for you, Pak." Kenny's icy tone sliced through the air. Pak did not flinch.

"Why are you doing this?" Ricco urged.

"I was sent to kill you." He stated the words so succinctly, Kenny wanted to blow the man's head off where he stood.

"What are you talking about? And besides, you had plenty of time to do it. Why am I still alive?" Ricco asked, seemingly trying to make some sense of his words.

"Ricco!" Kenny wanted her to shut up. The man was getting agitated and he was trying to keep him calm. He didn't want him to do something rash because he was distressed.

Kenny ignored the cutting look from her. No doubt she thought he was chastising her like a child.

"Who sent you to kill me?"

Kenny gritted his teeth, rage pumping through his veins.

"You're going to die, Pak, if you don't lower your weapon." Kenny told the man.

The malevolent smile that spread across Pak's face, let Kenny know that the man was willing to die to fulfill his mission. Kenny felt defenseless with no

248

weapon. All he could think to do was get between her and Pak.

"I was hoping you didn't die in the fire. I wanted the chance to toy with you. To play with you as if you were a rag dollie."

"Did you set the fire?" Kenny asked.

"No, fires are not my style?"

If he didn't do it, who did? Pak didn't take his eyes off of Ricco, not giving Kenny an opportunity to rush him. The man aimed the gun in one hand and slowly began to circle around them. He stopped in front of the cracked door. Pak took careful aim, Kenny saw him about to squeeze the trigger. Kenny leaped in front of the gun and Ricco, she screamed and the closet door flew open, knocking Pak to the ground and the gun from his hands.

Kenny scrambled for the gun. From the corner of his eye he saw Ricco run from the room. He was relieved she was no longer in harm's way. When he grabbed the gun and held it on Pak, he finally acknowledged the tall thin man pinning Pak onto his stomach.

"Ian?"

"Yes!" He answered.

A moment later, Cliff and Ted burst in the room with their weapons drawn. Ted grabbed Ian and threw him against the closet door. Kenny and Ricco both yelled, "No! He's on our side!"

Cliff made a call as to not have the Boston PD spread all over the neighborhood. The neighborhood didn't need anything else sensationalized in the news. A couple of agents arrived shortly after the call and quietly took Ye-Jun Pak into custody.

The last few days for them had been a whirlwind, to put it mildly and very revealing. And they had yet to make it to the hospital. However, things could have been much worse if Ian had not been there.

He'd said that he was getting dressed in the walk-in closet when he heard someone enter the condo. Thinking it may have been Ricco, he stayed in the closet to hurry and dress. Ricco must have come in right after Pak. When Ian hadn't heard anything, he peeked from the closet and saw the man holding a gun on Ricco.

It took nearly two hours for them all to be questioned by another agent who arrived after the first two. Kenny was certain that Cliff would have more information on Pak, before the end of the night.

"Do you miss working for the Bureau?" Kenny asked his friend.

Cliff looked up at him. "Feels like I never left. Hanging out with you, keeps me sharp." Cliff chuckled.

"So was that the development? That you know Ricco's true identity?" Kenny asked his friend.

"No."

"Then what is it?"

Cliff paused, his eyes serious, and he sensed Cliff struggled with what he had to say.

"What is it Cliff? He looked around to make sure Ricco wasn't in the room. "Is it Symphony?"

"It's about Frances."

Kenny felt like he'd been punched in the ribs. Frances? What development could there be about Frances?

With words he didn't recognize as his own, he finally asked, "What about Frances?"

"She's alive."

Chapter 28

A miracle by definition is: *an extraordinary and welcome event that is not explicable by nature or scientific laws and is therefore attributed to a divine agency.*

Ricco did not know by what divine force or agency protected a little girl in a building that crumbled all around her from an explosion, left her lying under a pile of rubble for days, and brought her out whole. She did not know—would never know, but the news of Frances broke Kenny in two. It was like he hated himself more because he didn't make certain if she had survived or not before leaving the area.

Grief distorted his mind, she knew that, because if he'd been thinking clearly he would have known it was impossible for him to return. He had also been injured from the explosion and there was nothing he could have done. All she could do was be there for him, though she did not know how much she helped.

Frances was a miracle.

He would see that one day.

It had been four days since finding out about Frances and though Kenny's world seemed to stand still while he processed Frances's survival, the rest of the world moved on.

Four days held, ninety-four hours, five thousand seven hundred sixty minutes, and three hundred forty-five thousand six hundred seconds.

On the fifth day, like winter lightning— unexpected, foreboding, and beautiful—the day held hidden miracles.

Just like with Frances, Ricco also didn't know what divine agency allowed a blackened angry sky to suddenly clear to a perfect blue as a surprisingly large crowd of onlookers listened to the beautiful notes of the flutes and strings echoing against the precipitous calm. They watched a precious two-year old wiggle her fingers goodbye as her mother's beautiful mahogany casket slowly lowered beneath the surface.

Kyle was inconsolable.

Days ago when the surgeon delivered the news to her closest family and friends that they'd done all they could to save her, Kyle was knocked to his knees. Ricco had never seen grief so raw and all-consuming, not even her own.

Symphony's funeral was held in St. Augustine, Florida where she'd lived most of her life. People from all over came to show their respects. Both of her bakeries were inundated with flowers, cards, trinkets, stuffed animals, and people lining up for blocks to buy the baked goods she'd created. In Boston, there was a rally. So many people gathered wearing pastel green T-shirts with the Symphony's logo to look like her famous pastry boxes.

They wanted justice.

The community wanted justice for Symphony James Dean, because she was a part of them, even for just a short time, and they wanted the killer found and justice served.

Neighbors had been questioned. A woman reported that she'd seen a figure running from the door after the shot had been fired. None of the door cameras were useful. The homes that had one, were too far from where Symphony and Kyle lived to pick up anything substantial. The police had nothing to go on. They had no idea if it was a random shooting or if she'd been the target.

At any rate, instead of the murder frightening the residents, they became more resilient. They were determined nothing or no one would run them out of their neighborhood.

Ricco included.

She'd lost her boss and the only friend she'd ever had. And like the rest of the neighbors, she refused to be bullied out of her home or place of employment. So far, Kyle had made no decisions about the bakeries. Ian was running the one in St. Augustine and Ricco ran the bakery in Boston as well as the commercial business. Though miles apart, she and Ian worked the business well together. They'd added their own touches here and there, but vowed to never let the soul of Symphony's die. So, as they each commanded their own kitchens, the music she loved still filled the spaces.

On the day of the funeral, Ricco and Kenny learned that Ye-Jun Pak was extradited to Japan. He'd been hired to kill her over seven years ago, but had only found her since she moved to Boston. She'd felt extremely vulnerable and violated at hearing the news. That someone had wanted to kill her had shaken her more than she wanted to admit. She'd been relieved that Kenny wanted to spend so much time with her. She didn't want to be alone.

"Are you almost ready?" Flour flew in the air as she spun around to the sound of the voice. She clutched her chest and spouted out some words in Japanese. "You startled me!"

"I'm sorry." Kenny walked towards her. "I knocked on the door before I entered, but I guess you couldn't hear me over the music."

She picked up a remote and lowered the volume. "Sorry, I had it turned up. I was missing her today."

"Is that why you're crying?"

"No. You scared a tear from my socket." She swiped at the tear. She hit his chest with a flour-covered hand."

"Heeyy! I'd planned on taking you to dinner in this shirt."

"Oh yeah. What about this face." She covered his face with flour. "Had you planned on bringing this face too?" She pulled him close and kissed him thoroughly.

"Well…I'd planned on it, but seems like you have better things in mind."

She gave him one more super loud kiss. "And I was ready, now I have to clean this up." She reached for a towel and wiped the counter. "What has you in such a good mood?" For the past few days, even when he was laughing there was always a hint of sadness lingering behind his beautiful vivid silver eyes, but not tonight. Tonight he seemed genuinely happy.

"I've decided to let go of the past and focus on my present and future."

She simply stared at him. Not sure what all that meant. "What does that look like?" She repeated the words he'd once spoken to her.

"It looks like us living our lives on *our* terms, because it doesn't matter how much we say we aren't going to let others predict our steps, we're still going to be looking over our shoulders. Because we know that somewhere in the background someone may be watching and plotting to do us harm."

"No one is plotting harm on you, I'm the one they're after."

"But don't you know, that harming you, would kill me." She thought of Kyle. Could Kenny really feel so strongly about her?

She wanted to believe him. She wanted to be the woman he claimed and loved. She wanted to be his peace. She wanted all those things, because she was in love with Kenny Cavanaugh. From the moment they'd met, he'd been haunting her, teasing her. That night he'd held her so lovingly and chased away her fears, he was solid and affirming. She felt the tiniest of pieces of her soul slipping back into place, but the very next day, the shelter and strength of his arms and presence turned into a puff of smoke—just an illusion that had rattled her and cracked her ability to trust just a little bit more.

"I won't."

"What?" She asked.

"I know what you were thinking. I told you why I did what I did. I will not hurt you again, Naricco, I couldn't."

"How can I be certain?"

"How can I be certain that one day you won't walk away from me, from us? Or heaven forbid…" He didn't finish his statement, and like she had been earlier, she knew he was thinking of the hell Kyle was going through right now. She knew Symphony and Kyle loved each other very much, but she was still taken away from him. Ricco realized there were no guarantees in life. A person just had to live the best they could, love all the ways they knew how, and stack up the memories for as long as they were able.

"I know." She finally voiced.

She thought of John standing in her bedroom holding a gun. She remembered when Kenny shielded her when he thought the man would shoot her. Love reveals itself in many ways and at that moment, she wanted to trust that life would give her many opportunities for her to reveal her love for Kenny.

"I don't know what evil may still be lurking out there to harm me, but I will let you love me for as long as you will and I will love you for as long as you will let me." To Ricco, love was more than an emotion, it was coupled with action that conveyed itself in ways noticed and unnoticed by the receiver. "Now, about this dinner you promised."

He pulled her close in a tight embrace and his ragged words next to her ear made everything alright.

"I love you so much, Naricco."

A lump formed in her throat and tears spilled from her eyes. "I love you back."

"Come on. I want you to grab an overnight bag from your place and then I'll feed you."

Confusion greeted him. "Why am I bringing an overnight bag to dinner?"

"Because dinner is at my place."

This was the first time he'd invited her to his place. She didn't even know where he lived. "And you're cooking?"

He grabbed at his heart. "You sure know how to wound a guy."

"That wasn't my intention. Just thought you were more of the breakfast and lunch kind of cook. Dinner is so domestic."

"So, more the guy to build the kitchen than to cook in it?"

"Not even that. You seem too polished and sophisticated to work outside all day. More the guy to design the kitchen, than to build it."

Grabbing at his chest again, he staggered backwards. "Damn, woman you definitely know how to slice a man open."

She laughed at his antics, yet another side of him she'd not seen before. Holding up her hands in surrender she said, "I will go home, shower, pack said bag, and let you dazzle me with your domestic dinner skills."

From the electric currents shooting from his gaze, dazzling her with his domestic skills was exactly what he had in mind.

Chapter 29

It was early evening, the sun and dusk created a vivid display towards the horizon. The beauty of the evening, the prospect of bringing Ricco home, and her soft scent filling the cab of his truck, had Kenny's body humming the entire drive.

If her mouth falling wide open when he pulled into his circular drive at his place was any indication, he predicted she was impressed by his home. He'd never brought a woman to his place. Not that he had a rule against it, he just had never met anyone that he'd wanted to share his private space with.

"Kenny this is beautiful."

His chest filled with pleasure at her reaction. He'd built the home two years ago. Since working with Ethan and Landon on the revitalization project, he'd fallen in love with New England. There was a different heartbeat here, a different soul that he hadn't picked up on anywhere else. It was a big city with a small town feel, bursting with history and a vitality that he'd grown to love.

"Thank you."

"Did you design it?"

He gave her an amused grin. "Designed and built it with my own two hands."

"How could those same hands build all of this and caress me so gently."

She had no idea she was in jeopardy of getting caressed and more, right in his truck if she didn't stop making comments like that. "Talent."

She rolled her eyes.

"It is beautiful." She said again. "Business must be good." But before he could respond, she rushed to say, "I'm sorry, Kenny, that was crass of me to say."

He waved her off. He didn't mind. His business was much better than good. It was a multimillion dollar kind of good. His company built most of the million dollar homes in New England and all over the country and with his partnership with Enrich Corp., the company owned by Ethan, Landon, and Joshua, and his investments, he was quite the wealthy man.

Kenny took in his home with fresh eyes. He had to admit, it was quite spectacular. At nearly five thousand square feet, sitting on a two-acre lot, it's large glass windows, with its modern architecture, and rustic touches, it truly was impressive.

"But, thank you. I'm very proud of it."

"As you should be."

"Would you like to spend the rest of your life in it?" He had not expected to say those words, but once they were out of his mouth, he didn't want to take them back. He wanted to spend the rest of his life with her and if she didn't like this house, he'd build her another—however and wherever she wanted.

She stilled, and his heart stopped. She turned to him and blinked. She stared at him for such a long time, he feared he was pushing her too far too fast. But then she spoke.

"What happened to your promise of building me a house just like Dixon and Gloria Phoenix's?"

His heart started up again and he gave her the sexiest smile he could muster. I will. Just tell me which coast in this world you want it on.

She laughed.

He didn't.

"You're serious?"

"I am."

"Kenny, I can't decide something like that on a whim." Crestfallen, he nodded. "I need to research where the best beaches are, but in the meantime, this will do just fine."

Turning off the ignition, he got out, and walked to her side of the car. He would not question her about side-stepping his proposal, once again. Instead, he pulled her out and lifted her into his arms. He kissed her softly before bringing her to the front door.

Without placing her on her feet just yet, he whispered, "How do you know this one will do? You haven't seen it yet."

Her large almond shaped dark eyes were shy as she looked up at him, "It will do, because you are here, Kenny San."

His heart swelled.

Dinner was delicious. Ricco knew he was a decent cook from the time she spent with him in South Carolina, but the meal he'd prepared for her tonight, was simply exquisite. The meal came with a set table and lit candles. She felt so cared for. The conversation flowed smoothly and they both were relaxed.

"That was delicious, Kenny. I think I may keep you around a while." She thought back to what he'd said before they got out of the car. *"Would you like to spend the rest of your life in it?"* If she didn't know any better, she'd thought it was a real marriage proposal. Was it?

He hadn't let her help with dinner, but she couldn't wait to get unleashed in his kitchen. It was a baker's dream. Double ovens, tons of counter space, a huge walk-in pantry, and every appliance she would ever need. The windows in the kitchen overlooked a small lake. "What a great view. Do you ever eat out on the patio."

"I sure do. Do you want to sit out there now?"

She did, but wondered how to get out there. All she saw was a solid wall of windows. "Yes. Do you get to the patio from the family room."

"You can, but we can go out right here too."

He pushed a switch on the wall and what she thought were just windows, was actually a patio door that folded like an accordion and gently slid back.

"Wow." She wondered what other wonders lay throughout his home. With the doors open wide, the patio became an extension of the kitchen eating area.

They sat on the most exquisite set of patio furniture she'd ever seen. Everything in his home screamed of wealth. Nothing was flashy or overt, but she knew this type of comfort came with a healthy price tag. She was not used to such luxuries and at times felt a bit overwhelmed by them.

He pulled her close and she'd never been more content in her life. "Are you ready to talk about it?" She felt him take in a deep breath.

"Yes."

"Tell me. What did Cliff have to say about Frances?"

"Do you remember the message that you decoded for me that first day I saw you on the island?"

"Yes. It read, 'muryō no mono,'" she turned slightly to look up at him, "the free one."

"Yes."

"Do you know who sent it?"

"She sent it."

"Why was the code translated to Nihongo?"

"Nihongo?"

"Why was it translated in the Japanese language?"

"Apparently, that's where she's been since right after I liberated her and left her to die in that building."

"I thought we were moving on?" She asked gently." He squeezed her in reply. When he didn't offer anything else, she asked, "Do you know how she was rescued?"

She was found by a group of insurgents and sold to a Japanese family seeking a kid."

"Oh no." She gasped.

"Actually, I think she may have been better off. Her father was a demon, who dealt in everything from drug and counterfeit goods smuggling, to sex trafficking. He was a murderer and it was said that he funded many terrorist groups."

266

"He hired you?"

"Yes."

"Why would you work for such a man?"

"I did it for Frances. My plan was to locate her then hand her over to a group I know who shelters children from unfit homes."

"Like Child Protective Services?"

"Yes, but better. These people do what's in the best interest of the child, but without all the bullshit."

"Your plan was to take her away from her father even though he'd hired you to 'liberate her?'"

"Yes." There was a hard, almost dangerous edge to his tone.

"Who had her?"

"She'd been kidnapped by a radical group determined to use her for leverage. They knew her father had the means to stop and end the civil war, either by force or his political influences."

"How did he know of you?"

"He didn't exactly. He knew the right people to get the right people to rescue his daughter."

"So, even though she was sold, she ended up in a good place."

"As far as we know."

"Where is she now?"

"We're trying to find out."

"How do you know her father isn't still trying to punish you for her so-called death?"

"He is dead."

"How do you know?"

"He is dead."

The finality of the statement made the hairs on the back of her neck stand.

Kenny Cavanaugh had a dark side.

Tucked comfortably in his arms with the sounds of the night surrounding them, she wondered about the depth of the darkness and if it was something she was ready to live with.

Chapter 30

Two weeks passed and there was still no clue as to who killed Symphony. It was heartbreaking to watch Kyle descend helplessly into the ongoing nightmare of the case that seemed not to have a resolution.

Again, Ricco and Kenny developed a routine. They stayed at her place during the week and his on the weekends and whenever she had a day off. It was quite a bit different than when they were on the island. On the island she'd admitted to herself that she loved Kenny, but was convinced after she went back to Boston, she would have to lock her feelings away. Now, she was beginning to believe that she no longer had to lock her love away in her heart.

She loved his place. It had all the modern conveniences they could need, but it was also warm and felt like a home. It was the first time she'd remembered feeling like that since she left her home in Japan, just over ten years ago.

For some reason, Kenny insisted on dropping her off at work this morning. They'd stayed at his place last night and would most likely stay at hers tonight. So, she didn't fuss. There was no place she needed to go, today. She'd just walk home. The

269

neighborhood was already awake with the delicious aromas of bread baking, mingling with gourmet coffees filling the air. This was her morning to come in late. The others had already gotten the bakery going and open.

"Do you mind if I walk in with you? I think I left some notes in the office."

"Nope." She knew it was his way of making an excuse of coming in to get pastries. He claimed they were for the office, but she wondered how much he actually shared.

He parked in front of the bakery, they got out, and she waited while he opened the door. When she stepped into the dining area, she waved to some of the customers she recognized and stopped to speak to one of her favorite customers who had the cutest little boy. He always reached for her to pick him up and this morning was no different. She picked up the little boy and talked to him for a few moments.

Jackson and Kim were working the counter as usual. They looked at her oddly.

"What are you doing here?" It was Jackson who asked.

She knew she was a few minutes later than normal but they knew she came in most days. "Same as you. Everything ok?" Kim was about to say something else when a customer walked up to the counter.

She shrugged, stepped into the kitchen, and froze. Ian was working on the large orders she'd prepped the night before.

"Ian!" Shocked to see him in her kitchen. "What on earth are you doing here?"

"I'm running the store while you're away."

"Away?" She placed her hands on her hips. "Where am I supposed to be going?"

Ian casually pointed over her shoulder and went back to work. There was a conspiratorial gleam in his eyes. Which was definitely out of character for him "Ask him."

Ricco spun around to Kenny and found him on one knee with a lit cupcake in his hand.

"Happy birthday, Naricco. And by the way, will you marry me?"

Struck completely dumb, Ricco's hands went to her mouth and tears immediately sprang from her eyes.

"What?" Elation, confusion, and something unnamed broke inside of her. She did not notice when Ian and the other workers quietly left the space, giving them privacy. She shook her head from side to side in sheer wonder at how magnificently perfect this man was to her and could not stop the tears from rolling uncontrollably down her cheeks. To Kenny, it must have looked like a refusal to his question, because he stood and immediately began to apologize.

"I'm sorry Ricco. I'm sorry. I know this is a lot. All of this. What happened on the island, Symphony, us spending so much time with each other." He paused seemingly searching for the words to make everything alright.

"No, Kenny. That's not why I'm crying." She stepped towards him. "I just can't believe that you're so incredible and that you want *me*."

"Want you? Naricco, I need you. I can't breathe when you aren't near. My life is not whole unless you are in it." He placed the cupcake on the counter and cupped her face. "Yes, I want you. I love you and I always want to be with you, through whatever comes at us."

"How did you know it was my birthday?"

"That's your question?"

"One of them."

"I know you Naricco Maki."

"But Naricco's birthday is in February."

"But Akiko's birthday is today. And that birthday is what was celebrated by your parents, your grandparents, and everyone else you loved and loved you. I wanted to be counted in that number."

She stood on her toes and kissed him in the middle of the kitchen—needing him, wanting to drown herself in the taste of him. He was the most delicious treat that had ever come out of the kitchen. "Thank you." He picked up the cupcake and held it up to her again. She blew out the candle immediately. No need for her to make a wish. And as if she'd forgotten all about him, she asked, "What's Ian doing here."

"There was a question posed after I wished you happy birthday."

She remembered the proposal and the tears fell again.

"You're killing me slowly here, Naricco."

"Which name do you prefer…Naricco or Akiko?"

He took a deep exasperated breath, "As long as it's followed by Cavanaugh, I don't care what your first name is."

"Then I shall be Naricco Cavanaugh."

Startled by his sudden yell, she was caught off guard when he swooped her into his arms and called up the stairs for Ian. "Ian, you are the best! We'll see you soon. Naricco will be back for her shift Tuesday morning.

Ian stood at the top of the stairs, "Congratulations, Ricco and happy birthday."

Before she could respond and question how he'd come to be in Boston, Kenny had whisked her from the shop and placed her into the truck.

"Where are we going?"

"To the airport."

Stunned, she turned to him. "The airport!"

"Yep."

"But I have no luggage, I'm in my work clothes."

"All minor details, my love."

He started the car and as he'd said, headed to the airport.

"Do you mind if I stop by my office? I need to grab a surprise for you."

"I'm not going to turn down a surprise."

Something foreign bubbled up inside of her as she watched the cars pass and the people walking along the streets going about their daily lives. Some wore expressions of seriousness, some no expressions at all, but there were a few who walked with a different step. They looked happy. Then she recognized the foreign feeling. It was happiness. She was genuinely happy.

Ricco reached for Kenny's hand, squeezed it, and smiled. She felt his gentle squeeze back as he turned into the garage of one of the larger buildings downtown.

"Is your office in this building?"

"Yes. Someone is going to bring it down for me."

"What?"

"Your surprise."

And just as he said it the elevator doors in the garage opened and a well-dressed man stepped out with a box in his hand.

"Just put it in the backseat, Drew."

Drew put the thing in the backseat and stepped to the driver's side door. She strained to see if she could tell what could be in the box. She couldn't.

"Sir." Drew looked to Ricco and hesitated.

He must be Kenny's assistant, she thought.

"What is it, Drew?"

"Just after you called saying you were going to stop by, someone has been waiting for you and refuses to leave until you arrive."

"A client?"

"I don't think so, sir."

Ricco noticed how he kept glancing at her. "I'll wait for you if you have to go up to the office, there's a few phone calls I want to make since apparently I'll be out of town for a few days." She said.

Kenny was anxious to get out of town with Ricco. He'd purposely not gone into work today for the mere fact that he didn't want to get tied up into anything. He had no idea who could be waiting for him and refusing to leave. He should have told Drew to tell whomever it was that he'd already gone.

"Where is he?" Kenny asked Drew.

"She's in the lobby, sir."

So they took the elevator up to the lobby level. Kenny saw security talking to a young woman and walked over.

"I don't know what she wants, but she sure is pretty, isn't she." Drew's words vaguely registered with Kenny. He was too busy trying to figure out who the young woman was and why she was there. He didn't think she was a client, but then his business had grown so large, he no longer knew all his clients personally.

He walked up to the two security guards hovering over the woman who looked to be more girl than woman. She was just a teenager.

"What's going on?" He asked, frowning. The young woman stood.

"I'm Kenny Cavanaugh. How may I help you?"

"You're Kenny Cavanaugh?"

"Yes." He frowned. He felt like he should know who she was. There was something about her that was vaguely familiar. "Yes, I'm Kenny Cavanaugh. And you are?"

"I am Kim Ito."

The name was not familiar to him at all. He turned to Frank and Landry, "I got it from here, guys."

"You sure, Mr. Cavanaugh?" One of them asked. He wasn't sure which. Kenny was too busy wondering about Kim Ito and why she was looking for him.

"Yes."

The men, including Drew, walked away and left him alone with Kim.

"Would you like to go to my office or can we talk here?" He was hoping she didn't want to go to his office, he didn't want to leave Ricco in the car for too long.

"I will not keep you, Mr. Kenny."

Kenny stilled.

There was only one person who'd ever called him that. His eyes widened and he staggered back a step. "Frances?" The name coming out wrapped in emotions Kenny couldn't name.

"Yes. I am the little girl you taught to be brave."

277

Not believing what was happening, Kenny shook his head in wonder. For several long moments, he stared at her. He saw the scar her remembered along her jaw and new scars on her forehead near her right temple and wondered if she'd gotten them from the explosion.

From somewhere he found common courtesy and offered her a seat.

"I know you're wondering why I'm here."

Finding it difficult to breathe, he answered her truthfully. "Yes. I am. I've only recently found out you were alive."

"I found out how to find you from someone who used to work for the man that was once my father." Kenny thought that odd for her to say, but remembered she was raised by new parents. He also wondered how the man knew his true name. The only person he'd ever given it to, was Frances. "He had been working for your government, even when he claimed to work for the man I was born to. He discovered your identity and told me that Kenny Cavanaugh was the man who saved my life. I wanted to thank you. He also helped me send you a message. I really don't know how he was going to do it without anyone finding out, but he assured me he would."

"I got the message, but wasn't sure what it meant. How could you think I saved your life? I left you in that building. You could have died." Kenny looked around to make sure no one was listening to their conversation and now wished he would have brought her up to his office after all. "I thought you were dead." His last words were jagged and seemed to rip open all the old wounds he'd thought were healed.

"But I didn't. If the building hadn't blown up, I would have been sent back to the man who hired you to rescue me. I was not afraid of the explosion. I was afraid of a father who'd murdered people in front of me, thinking it would make me admire him."

"I had no intentions on leaving you with that monster." She looked confused and he explained his plan of taking her away from her father.

Her lips curved into a sad smile as tears filled her eyes. Even now he wanted to take her in his arms and keep her safe. She'd grown into a beautiful young lady. By his calculations, she'd turned sixteen only a few months ago.

Soon a couple approached them. Kenny assumed they were her parents. Wiping her tears, she smiled and embraced them both. Kenny stood. "Hello, I'm Kenny Cavanaugh."

"We know." The woman closed his hand in both of hers. Her English was framed in a very thick Japanese accent. "Thank You." She turned to Frances, "Come Kim, we must go."

They all turned to him with grateful eyes, bowed, then walked away. The tightness in his throat made him afraid to speak, so he just nodded and bowed in return.

Chapter 31

"How are you?"

For the past ten minutes, his only words had been, "It was Frances. She was the person waiting for me."

A hundred questions ran through Ricco's head, but she could tell he was trapped in the past at the moment. His profile was rigid and it broke her heart to see him this way.

"Kenny?"

"She's sixteen years old now." His voice barely above a whisper. The sadness coating each word made her take a closer look at him.

"Was she upset with you?"

"No." She was confused by the disgust in his tone. "She'd wanted to find me to thank me for convincing her that bravery lived inside of her."

"And you're upset by that?"

"You just don't understand."

He was right. She didn't. She also resented the fact that he was determined to hang on to a hurt that no longer had any validity. Frances was not dead as he'd assumed for the past ten years. She was alive and attributed her life to him. She sounded like a remarkable young lady.

She reached to stroke his shoulder and slid her hand up the back of his neck. He was tense.

Enough of this, she thought.

She stroked the back of his neck again, sliding her hand up and politely shoved him in the head. The truck swerved sharply and he ducked out of her reach.

"What the hell was that for?"

"For you! You're an idiot."

She was tired of his sulking and didn't care if this would ignite their first official fight as an engaged couple. His knuckles were white as he gripped the wheel. He shifted angry eyes to her then back on the road.

"She's *sixteen* years old, Kenny." He stiffened and she placed a gentle hand on his forearm. "*Sixteen*."

"What's your point, Naricco?"

"My point is, Kenny," she punctuated his name with the same hint of irritation that accompanied hers. "That she is sixteen years old, because you taught her to be brave. She is sixteen years old, because she was raised by good parents. She is sixteen years old." She took a deep breath before saying her next words. "What she is not, Kenny, is a memory of a dead six year old." He flinched at that last statement. Squeezing his arm she wanted him to realize that because of him, she was a teenager. "You liberated her, Kenny. I know it. She knows it. The only person who doesn't seem to know it, is you." Moving her hand, she smacked him in the head again. "Now, get your shit together and stop acting like a moping child!" It was something Symphony would have done and said if she were here and for that, she was proud of herself.

With folded arms Ricco sat back in her seat and looked straight ahead. They rode in silence like that for another few minutes. Her irritation was so thick it cast its own shadow. What the hell was his problem. Not even an hour ago, they were both glowing with happiness. He'd asked her to marry him and was whisking her away for a long weekend. She wasn't about to let him sulk for no reason at all. Like she'd told him a few moments before, he'd better get his shit together!

His gentle laughter rippled through the air. She couldn't help but turn towards it. He still kept his eyes on the road. Curse her stupid mouth for forming into a smile. Quickly pursing her lips she huffed and turned to look out of the passenger window.

"I'm sorry, Naricco." His words coaxed her to turn his way again. "You're absolutely correct. I do need to get my shit together."

"How are you?" She began again, hoping for a different response.

"I was just so surprised to see her, Naricco."

Still not looking at him, she said, "I imagine that must have been a shock."

"Yes, it was." He paused for so long that she was certain he wouldn't answer. "I could still see the brave six year old in her eyes."

From the window, Ricco saw the signs directing them to the airport garage. Without turning towards him she said simply, "And she's sixteen, now."

"Yes, she is." She could hear the smile in his reply.

Finally, she thought. He would be alright. They would be alright.

Both times they'd flown before she'd been too dazed to wonder how or why they were in a private plane.

Today, she had questions.

"You must have some pretty powerful friends to be able to keep borrowing their private jet. Does it belong to the Phoenixes." She knew they were really close friends as well as business associates. She hadn't really before, but she took the time to look around at the spacious interior.

The plane could accommodate at least ten people very comfortably. Its soft tan leather seats were a perfect complement to the dark wood trim and white bulkheads. Whomever owned the plane must be very wealthy. It was designed to both entertain for business and pleasure and be comfortable for long trips. She was positive there was a bedroom behind the door at the back of the cabin.

"I don't mean to be nosey, but who owns this plane?" Her eyes traveled the length of him. Even in jeans and a t-shirt he dripped with refinement, masculinity, and handsomeness so sharp it made her heart ache.

"It's mine and when we marry, it will be yours as well."

"Wha-what?" She stuttered and looked around the spacious cabin. Her mind was racing a mile a minute. She never imagined herself with such luxury and it was difficult for her to imagine it now. "Why do you need a private jet?"

"My business takes me all over the world, Naricco."

"Your construction business?"

"Yes, but I'm also a well sought after architect."

"I thought only extremely rich people had private jets—like millionaires."

"That's probably a true statement."

She just stared at him. From his home and the business he owned, she figured him to be quite well off, but this…this was something different altogether.

In slow, controlled words, she asked, "So, you're a millionaire?"

"Is that a problem?"

Was it? She didn't think so. The situation had never come up. She'd gone on a few dates over the years, but all the guys worked at either restaurants near the beach or at one of the hotels in the area. Once she'd dated a guy who'd been visiting St. Augustine on business from Orlando. He drove to see her a few times before she broke it off with him, for no other reason than because they didn't seem to have much chemistry.

"It's never come up."

"Well…" He began with genuine concern in his eyes. She just stared at him. "I guess I also better mention that the building we went to today is mine as well."

Her eyes went round. "The whole building?"

"Yes." And again he asked, "Is that a problem?"

Again she asked herself if him being wealthy was an issue with her.

No. It wasn't. She loved him. It was as simple as that. With a smile peeking out, she said, "I guess I can learn to live with it." Her brows bunched as a thought suddenly occurred to her "You won't be expecting me to quit my job will you?"

"Would you ever want to run your own bakery?"

"I could never leave Symphony's. She gave me my first job when I came to St. Augustine."

"What brought you to St. Augustine, of all places when you fled Japan?"

I'd read somewhere that it was the oldest city in the United States and it also had a college. Somehow I thought it would remind me of home, because of all the ancient traditions in Japan."

"Did it?"

"Not even a little bit, but I came to love it as much."

"What about Boston."

"I was apprehensive about moving to Boston, but I couldn't turn down Symphony after all she'd done for me."

"Why were you apprehensive?"

"Because the first time I came, I got my heart broken." She could see the pain, shame, and regret play across his features. "But now…" She paused. "But now, I realize I can live anywhere as long as you are there too."

The pilot announced that it was safe to remove their seatbelts just in time for him to pull her into his lap and make her forget she'd ever had her heart broken by him.

Chapter 32

"You brought me to LA? How long was I asleep?" She asked as the driver drove them away from LAX.

"Yep. You slept for about two hours."

"Why did you bring me to Los Angeles?"

"Because I can." He was enjoying keeping her in suspense. He wanted to give her a romantic weekend away, where she could relax, take her mind off of missing her friend, and honestly, he just wanted her all to himself.

Everywhere they'd been, there'd been distractions, to say the least. Boat explosions, Symphony's murder, and Pak showing up at her condo made him realize that he wanted to grasp every moment he could with her.

He loved her.

Had loved her since the very first night. He'd blamed him wanting to go up to her hotel room that night on a strange infatuation or fixation, because of the sadness in her eyes, but the feeling hadn't waned no matter how hard he tried to ignore it. His heart literally ached for her.

When he found out she'd moved to Boston, he was angry. Mostly at himself, because he couldn't seem to stay away from her. Of course she had no idea, but he found ways to try and catch glimpses of her—riding by the shop, her home. Before he knew it, he'd become a full-fledged stalker. He'd blamed it on his notion of making sure she was safe. Someone may have seen them together that one day and think she was a love interest. Whatever he had to say to himself to not sound like a lovesick fool.

And now she'd agreed to be his wife. Kenny was over the moon with elation.

"Why LA?'

Her question brought him back to the present. "Why not?" He waggled his eyebrows. She was so beautiful. He saw the tiny eye roll and looked forward to her fiery spirit he would encounter in the bedroom later. "Are you tired?"

"Nah. I'm very well rested." She cocked her head and arched a brow, but it was the heat in her eyes that made his manhood stir. He was going to suggest a shopping trip before they got to their hotel, but maybe that could wait.

"Oh yeah? Come here." He reached for her and she came willingly. The soft nibbles he placed on her bottom lip only whet his appetite for something far more indecent than what they could do in a car. But that thought quickly faded when she parted her lips for him. Kenny lost himself in the haze of desire that held them both. His calm was shattered with the fervor in which she returned his kisses.

Kenny slid her into his lap and intended on exploring a lot more than her mouth.

"Excuse me, Mr. Cavanaugh. Mr. Cavanaugh!"

Kenny remembered where they were, releasing Ricco from his lap, but he still wasn't pleased about being interrupted. "What?" He growled, at the driver.

Not perturbed by Kenny's tone, the driver asked, "Do you still want to make that stop on Rodeo Drive?"

What he wanted to do was tell the man to do what he had to do to get them to the hotel as quickly as possible. Yes, he'd made love to Ricco before, but he'd never made love to her as his fiancé. But the irritation of being interrupted was quickly dispelled by Ricco's excitement. She actually bounced in her seat.

"We're going shopping on Rodeo Drive!"

Kenny looked at the driver, "Well, there's your answer. The lady wants to go shopping."

"Shopping on Rodeo Drive is on my bucket list. I think I may have saved enough to get me two complete outfits." She started looking out the windows to see if they were close to Beverly Hills yet.

Kenny frowned. Did she honestly think she would have to pay for her shopping spree? She must have.

"Naricco, this is my treat." Kenny saw the driver eye him through the rear view mirror and wanted to tell the man to mind his own business and keep his eyes on the road.

"I couldn't possibly let you do that." Kenny thought the determined set of her mouth was so cute.

"Yes you could and yes I will treat you to whatever you want." He turned to look directly at her. "Naricco, I will spoil you until your heart's content, this weekend." She blinked but said nothing. "And for the rest of your life."

"How am I supposed to repay you for all of this?" She waved her hands in the air.

"By loving me for the rest of my life."

"Kenny, I—" He cut her off with a kiss and he could feel her acquiescence in the way her lips softened and allowed themselves to be persuaded. He knew he could probably suggest anything right now and she would follow him like an obedient lamb.

"What were you saying?" He asked when he finally pulled away.

"Thank you."

He wasn't quite sure what she was thanking him for, but he would see if he could coax that kind of reaction from her later when they couldn't be disturbed.

Kenny was just as giddy as Ricco, watching her try on outfits. He had no idea how edgy she liked to dress. Most of the time when he saw her she'd been in her work clothes and any other time, she'd dress very conservatively. He loved her in anything, but he had to admit, she was stunning in the clothes she'd tried on and sexy as hell.

Three hours later and the car loaded with more packages than they could both carry, she gave him a hard squeeze around his waist. "Kenny, are you sure about all of this stuff?" She asked as she placed the last package with the rest.

"I know you Naricco. Even though I can afford for you to do this whenever you desire, that is not who you are. So, yes, please let me indulge you from time to time."

She stood on her toes and placed a kiss so sweet on his lips, it made his throat constrict. He loved her so much. The strength that lived inside of her made him want to take away every burden, every hurt, every single thing that may have caused her pain. "We have one more store to go to." He said, pulling her gently by the hand.

"I don't think I can try on one more thing. I'm tired of taking my clothes off and on."

"I'll take them off next time, and you won't have to worry about putting them back on for the rest of the weekend."

"Then where are we going?"

"You'll see. I want you to meet a friend of mine. He owns a store down the block."

"Well it's a good thing I wore the last outfit out of the store. At least now I'm presentable."

"Baby, you're always presentable." He saw her still as she stared up at him. "What?" Had he said something to upset her.

"That's the first time you've ever used an endearment when speaking to me." Her smile was shy and wistful. "I liked it."

Kenny squeezed her hand and they both walked toward his friend's store.

"Who's your friend?" She asked right before they arrived.

"Barron Yaeger."

She stopped again, her mouth agape. "Barron Yaeger? *The* Barron Yaeger?"

He shrugged. "I guess. To me, he's just been Barry. I've been knowing him since middle school. We met at summer camp one year and have been friends ever since. How do you know him?"

"I don't *know* him. I know *of* him. I've been salivating over his jewelry ever since the first time I've gotten my hands on an American fashion magazine."

Well, he thought, that's good news. Maybe this won't be as hard as he thought. A guard opened the door. "Welcome. Mr. Cavanaugh."

Kenny ignored the surprise in Ricco's eyes. They stepped just inside the door. Kenny turned to Ricco. "I hope this isn't too corny for you." His heart raced as he took a deep steading breath. "I've asked you to marry me and you said yes. Forgive me for not having the ring then, but to make up for it, you may choose anyone you like." He waved a hand towards the counters.

Surely she was dreaming.

She had to be dreaming.

This was just like a scene in the movies. There were well dressed sales people positioned all around the store, with rings displayed on each counter.

"Kenny I—"

"Yes, you can. Take your time." With his hand placed at the small of her back, he encouraged her to take a step forward. A tall impeccably dressed brown skinned man, approached them.

"You must be, Naricco. I've heard that you've made my friend here a very happy man."

"That she has." Kenny interrupted.

"It's a pleasure to meet you, Naricco. I am Barron Yaeger, but my friends call me Barry." He turned to Kenny with wonder in his eyes then back to her. "Kenny failed to tell me how beautiful you are. You know, he isn't all that great. Construction worker and all. I can give you diamonds."

"Don't listen to him, Naricco."

She could barely follow their teasing, she just hoped her mouth would function when she opened it. She could not believe she was meeting Barron Yaeger and that he was friends with Kenny! She'd been admiring his jewelry since she was twelve. Her mouth was dry, but she managed to form words. "It's nice to meet you too, Mr. Yaeger."

"Barry. Please." He corrected her.

"It's nice to meet you, Barry."

Before either of them could say anything else, Barry spoke to the guard. "Felix, she's here again." She and Kenny looked towards the window where a woman had her hands and face pressed to the glass admiring the jewelry displayed there. "My apologies. She's been coming here every day lately, lingering in the window. She will stay for hours if no one runs her off." Barry turned back to Ricco. "Now, would you like for me to show you around?"

Still too overwhelmed to speak, she just looked up at him and nodded. Looking over at Kenny, she noticed he was still looking at the woman in the window with the oddest expression on his face.

"Kenny, are you ok?"

He watched the woman walk away before turning to Ricco. "I'm sorry. But she looked very familiar. I was trying to figure out where I knew her from."

Ricco looked back to the window. The woman was gone. From the glimpse she'd gotten of her, she was a nice looking, light skinned, African American woman with a cute platinum pixie cut. Did he think she was someone he used to date? She quickly threw that thought away. He'd brought her to the most exclusive jewelry store on the West Coast, because he wanted to marry *her*, not anyone else. So damn that woman in the window, she was here to pick out her engagement ring.

Kenny couldn't help but love the joy he saw in Ricco's face. She seemed truly pleased and that thrilled him to no end. He'd thought maybe she would think all of this was over the top, but who would have known that she was a fan of Barry's work. He walked towards Ricco and Barry, but had a nagging feeling that he knew that woman. He looked again at the window. She was gone, of course.

Where did he know her from?

He couldn't shake the feeling that he'd not only seen her before, but knew her. There was something about the hair. He would have remembered her hair. Maybe the last time he saw her it was different.

Kenny pushed the woman out of his mind and focused on the woman he wanted to marry. He wondered if he could get her to marry him this weekend.

Chapter 33

Completely overwhelmed by everything that was Kenny Cavanaugh, she couldn't help the tears that ran unchecked down her cheeks. She looked around the beautiful Japanese inspired accommodations and couldn't believe he'd gone through so much trouble just for her.

"I feel like I am back home."

"I hope you feel good about that."

She stared at an exquisite suite of rooms that reminded her so much of Japan that for a moment she felt she was there. And for some reason, her thoughts of home didn't bring sadness to her soul. She felt uplifted and protected. She thought of her parents and knew they would be happy for her and wouldn't want her burdened with the sadness that's weighed on her so heavily since she was sixteen.

"I was afraid it would make you sad." She felt him at her back.

"No. I'm not sad." She turned towards him.

"But you're crying."

"They're happy tears."

"Then are you truly happy?"

299

Unable to speak she just nodded. He pulled her into his arms and like that very first time, she felt safe. It suddenly occurred to her that she hadn't had to try so hard to not count things. He truly was her place of peace. "I love you so much, Kenny."

"Will you marry me?"

She saw the ring on her finger as she wrapped her arms around his neck. It was perfect for her—a beautiful heart cut diamond on a thin platinum band. "This ring indicates I've already said yes."

The soft nibble on her lobe heated more than that ear. The rich vibration of his voice uttered, "This weekend."

She froze. What was he asking her? To marry her this weekend?

There were so many uncertainties in their lives, so many unknowns, but what she was absolutely sure about, was that she loved Kenny Cavanaugh. He was her peace and she was his. And that was all they needed to know. That was all the certainty they required.

"I will marry you, today if we could."

"How about tomorrow? We can get the license first thing in the morning and get married at sunset." He lifted her in his arms and walked her to the glass doors at the patio area, pressed a button and the doors pushed open to the length of the room. The patio was beautiful. They were right on the beach! He placed her on her feet and the view literally took her breath away. For a moment she felt like she had after the fire.

"Kenny." His name came out in astonishment. "This is…this is…" She couldn't seem to find the words.

"That's exactly how I feel."

She looked up and saw his eyes were on her instead of the stunning view of the pacific ocean and her heart ascended to a place she was excited to explore.

"We can get married right out there." She looked out where he pointed and couldn't wait to be his wife. "Is that ok? If you want all the bells and whistles, we can do that too. I'm willing to wait." His sullen face implied no such thing, but she didn't need to wait. She had no family and her only friend had been Symphony. "It's perfect, Kenny." She smiled up at him, gently touched his face and kissed him soundly. "Just perfect for us."

She walked the length of the deck and leaned against the rail there. She wanted her friend to rest in peace, but knew she wasn't, knowing that her murderer was still out there somewhere. She extended her hand to him and he came to her, her back sheltered into his front.

"What's wrong, Naricco?"

"Just thinking about Symphony. I know she would be happy for me, but I can't be at peace with her death, because I know she is still restless and wants us to find the killer."

"Do you want me to put Cliff on the case?"

"Maybe we should. I was trying to let the police do their job, but two weeks have passed. Two weeks that the killer has been out there thinking they've gotten away with taking my friend away from her husband, her baby, " she paused a beat, "from me, Kenny. She was my best friend. As short-lived as it was, she was my only friend."

She wanted to be blissfully happy for Kenny and herself, and in a way she was, but there was still the shadow of the unsolved murder of her friend lingering over them and she knew it would cling to them until they found out who killed her friend.

The strength of his hold comforted her and she hated to feel this way, but it couldn't take away her unease.

It was time.

Kenny took a deep calming breath, trying to slow his frantically beating heart. Closing his eyes he focused for a moment on the aroma of the salt mingling with the crisp California air. He always loved the beach. The coast in Washington had its own charms. He and his mom spent lots of time there during the summers, but nothing seemed to compare to the beaches of Southern California. Inhaling again, the fragrant aroma of the flowers covering the bower gave him a fresh sense of excitement and the feeling of freedom. Finally allowing himself to love Ricco was allowing him to shed all the dark places covering his heart. And in just a few moments in this very spot, he was waiting to marry her and they would become one.

He'd chosen this particular hotel because it offered its guests privacy. The horizon displayed bright orange and violet streaks that reflected subtly on the few clouds speckled above. It made for a perfect backdrop against the bower the hotel set up for the occasion.

He wanted to kick himself for suggesting sunset. Why couldn't he have said sunrise instead! It didn't take any time to get the license. They both smiled and giggled like idiots through the entire process.

They'd had a really nice lunch and another shopping trip to get clothes for the ceremony. She'd kept hers a secret, but insisted on helping him pick his. She was convinced a man should be married on the beach in cream colored slacks, white shirt, cream vest, and blue tie. He was able to choose any type of blue he wanted, but she liked the one with the cream colored thin stripes.

The officiant provided by the hotel had arrived along with the harpist, and a photographer. Kenny's eyes didn't stray far from their deck, he wanted them waiting there when she stepped out.

"Lovely sunset out this evening, isn't it son?" Kenny reluctantly turned to the older gentleman who was looking at the horizon.

"Yes it is." He replied, obviously distracted, as he quickly looked at the sunset then back at the deck.

He didn't hear the quiet knowing chuckle from the man or see anything else beyond the deck.

And there she was.

"Well, son, no wonder you aren't impressed with the sunset. It doesn't hold a candle to her."

Kenny couldn't respond to the man if he wanted to. He was struck dumb and completely paralyzed by the vision of his Naricco. Her beautiful strapless lace dress was the same cream color of his wedding attire, but it was the stunning blue obi around her waist that revealed her true Japanese exquisiteness. She was truly a vision. His Japanese beauty.

The harpist began to play as Ricco walked towards him. He couldn't believe this was happening and she'd agreed to be his wife. They hadn't known each other very long, but he felt like she knew the details of his soul and he knew hers. She never wore much makeup, but today she wore just enough to enhance her beauty rather than mask it. With her hair pulled back, her eyes were more striking than ever— black almond shaped windows that reflected love.

Love for him.

She loved him. She really loved him. Kenny inhaled deeply again, filling with pride that this woman was his future.

Instead of some fancy shoes, Ricco was glad she opted for the barefoot sandals the sales lady suggested. Beautiful straps encrusted with jewels, allowing her to walk on the soles of her feet. She was more nervous than she'd ever been in her life and was glad not to have to worry about balancing heels in this sand.

The future she faced with this man would be a journey they took with only one another. They had no family to lean on and therefore would have to rely on just each other. Would she be enough for him?

The music began. She squeezed the short stems of the beautiful bouquet of white roses she'd found on the bed with a beautiful note from Kenny. She figured they'd come from the box he'd gotten from the office.

Finally brave enough to look up at him, she found his eyes waiting and what reflected in them, set her soul at ease. He loved her. She was more certain of that than anything else she'd ever known.

Somehow she found herself standing at Kenny's side. She looked up at him and smiled. The smile that was returned unfurled any hurt and pains she'd known before and they flew off like a butterfly.

The officiant asked, "From what I understand, you may not have had time to prepare your own vows. Shall I use the standard ones?"

She looked up at Kenny. "I will just speak from my heart." There was nothing the officiant could recite that would come close to what she wanted to say.

"As will I." Kenny replied.

"Ok, well let's get on with it."

Whatever else the man said was a haze. Kenny had placed her hand in his and the contact immediately calmed her. She was so ready to marry this man. She turned to him waiting for the words that would bind them.

"Kenny Owen Cavanaugh do you take Naricco Maki as your lawfully wedded wife?"

"I certainly do."

Ricco beamed.

"Naricco Maki…" Ricco thought about the girl who was once Akiko Ishido and knew she could never leave her completely behind. It was the part of her that was connected to her parents, her grandparents, and the life she'd known in Japan. Her name was never legally changed to Naricco Maki. It is the name she created when she created a new life. Though her new identity had a social security number and birth certificate as if she was born in America. All the details had been worked out by Nanan and the people she knew. Ricco was uncertain how she'd been found in the States, although she knew nothing was truly secret anywhere.

"Naricco?" She heard the officiant ask. Snapped out of her musing, she looked up at the question in Kenny's eyes. "Oh…Yes!" She said hurriedly, "I do." She wanted to reassure him so she added, "I was thinking about my parents."

Kenny nodded.

They exchanged rings. He slipped a band of small heart shaped diamonds on her finger that beautifully matched her engagement ring. With trembling fingers, she placed a platinum band on his finger. She fingered her ring, not remembering seeing it in the jewelry store. Looking up at him in awe, she grinned at his mischievous wink.

Kenny liked surprising her.

It was time for their vows. She knew the words would come when it was her turn, but she was curious as to what Kenny would say to her.

"My Naricco, I vow to do my best to never be the cause of any sadness in your eyes. I know our parents are not present with us anymore, but I know they are happy for us and will be ever present in our lives. I vow to be your family, your best friend, your lover, your champion, your cheerleader, your helpmate, your food taster, and your place of peace for the rest of our lives. I promise to be true to you and never put you in a position where you have to question how much I love you. You will know it, Naricco. You will know it in the way that I speak to you, the way that I touch you, the way that I protect you from harm, because I love you today, tomorrow, and always no matter what comes our way."

The soft crash of the waves filled the moments they all needed after such a promise. She knew he could see the tears shining in her eyes. The officiant cleared his throat, seemingly to get his own composure together. He looked towards her and nodded for her to begin.

Taking a deep breath, she gathered her thoughts and looked into the silver eyes that had always taken her breath away. "Kenny Cavanaugh, I promise I will do my best to live up to the woman worthy enough to allow you to let down your guard and give love another chance. I promise to never make that ham sandwich you like for any other." He grinned and her heart felt light and free. "I promise to be your place of peace, the supporter of your dreams, and forever the love of your life, because you will forever be the love of mine. I will be true to you and promise to never give you a reason to question my love for you. Kenny, I will be your source of strength. I will proudly walk at your side through this journey of life." Her eyes never left his as she took a deep breath. Already the tears were falling and she felt the gentle squeeze of his hand again. "When I left Japan at the age of sixteen, my heart was trapped in a shadow of darkness and pain. That was, until I met you. Even when you were not ready to love again, you'd been a place of peace and safety for me. Even in this short time we have found each other again, we have overcome so much, braved obstacles others will never face, and proved that love has the last say. I love you Kenny Cavanaugh, and if we had to start this journey with one cent to our names, I will continue to do so, tomorrow, and for each day we are blessed to travel this world together."

Chapter 34

Sated and famished from their spirited wedding night, Kenny hated that he'd ordered room service to deliver breakfast so early. It was already 9 AM, but they had not even looked for sleep until the sky was losing its grip on the night.

He slid naked from the huge bed and grabbed a robe from the chair where he'd thrown it the night before. Turning back, he marveled that the tiny woman taking up so little space in the bed was actually his wife. He saw her reach for him, but saw she had not awakened.

He closed the bedroom door and headed to get breakfast. After everything was set on the table, he hesitated to wake her. He wanted to get back in bed with her and get to breakfast later, but knew everything would be cold by then. Deciding to see if she wanted breakfast he headed back to their bedroom. Picking up his phone along the way, he saw a few missed calls from Terry. It was noon on the east coast so he gave him a call before waking his wife. Oh how he liked the sound of that, even if it was just in his head.

He clicked Terry's number.

"It's about time. I was trying to get a fourth for poker last night." Terry said.

"I'm out of town."

"Oh. You hadn't mentioned it. I thought all of your out of town contracts were being handled by Skip?"

"They are. I'm away on pleasure." There was a pause on the line and Kenny knew Terry probably figured he was with Naricco, but wasn't so rude as to ask. "My wife and I are in California."

"Wife!"

As to put him out of his misery, he went ahead and told him who he was with. "Yes. Naricco and I were married yesterday evening."

To his surprise Terry didn't sound surprised by his revelation at all.

"Well I'll be damned. Congratulations, man!"

"Thank you."

"So you mean to tell me, you got up on the morning after your wedding night and called me. I'm flattered, but it doesn't bode well with how your wedding night was supposed to go.'

"For your information I'd just gotten up to let room service in. Ricco's still asleep and I checked my phone to give her another few minutes as she hasn't been asleep too long."

Terry laughed. "Alright man, whatever you say. I wish the two of you much happiness."

"We are happy, Terry. You should try it yourself."

"Trust me, I'm looking forward to getting married and starting a family, however, I'm missing an important ingredient in that recipe. Seems to me having a girlfriend is key to making that happen."

"I thought you and Ava were pretty hot and heavy?"

"We broke up a couple weeks ago. She quit…or at least she just never showed back up to work."

Kenny had no idea they were no longer an item. "Hey man, I'm sorry. I didn't know."

"I'm not. She was starting to get too weird about Symphony."

Kenny frowned. "What do you mean?"

"I mean, she was almost obsessed with her. She flew completely off the handle whenever Symphony was in the same room with me."

A thought struck Kenny with such a blow that he had to sit down. No, it must just be a coincidence. He shook his head with a very unwelcomed thought.

"You still there?" Terry asked.

"Do you know where Ava is?"

"Probably off somewhere trying to get some other man to marry her. Along with Symphony, she was obsessed about getting married. I mean, I had feelings for her, but she hinted around about marriage all the time. She talked about the type of ring she wanted."

"Oh God…" Kenny's brain scrambled to find the image of the woman in the window. The hair was short and a different color, but he was certain it was her. But why would she be in California looking so differently…unless. The thoughts running through his mind so sharply hit him like a punch in the gut.

"Terry you said you broke up with Ava two weeks ago?"

"Yeah? Why?"

"Was it before or after Symphony was killed?"

Terry paused for a long moment. "What are you getting at, Kenny? Do you think—"

Kenny's voice rose and became more urgent. "Was it before or after, Terry?"

"I've never really thought back to it, I was so torn up about Symphony." And Kenny could still hear the pain in his tone. "But now that you ask, I broke up with her when I took her home from Landon's in-law's anniversary party. She'd been exceptionally rude and nasty to Symphony that night and I'd had enough.

Later that night, is when I got word that Symphony had been shot."

"I think I saw her."

"Who?"

"Ava."

"Where?"

"In California."

And before Kenny could finish, Terry asked, "You saw Ava in California?"

"I didn't know it was her at the time. Her hair was different, but I was certain I knew the woman."

"Where were you?"

"I was at Barron Yaeger's."

"Oh my god."

There was something in Terry's tone that gave Kenny pause.

"What is it?"

"She talked about that jeweler whenever she could fit it in the conversation."

"Does Ava own a gun?"

"Yes."

Kenny cursed out loud—for several reasons. He was quite certain that Ava Fletcher killed Symphony. The other reason was he wasn't sure how the news would affect his wife.

"We need to alert the police, in Boston and in LA." Kenny stated. Terry agreed and quickly disconnected the call.

"I knew this weekend was too good to be true. We can't seem to go anywhere together without getting the police involved." It was Ricco emerging from the bedroom in a short red kimono style robe. Just the sight of her made his entire body come alive, but he knew that once he told her what he'd discovered, it would be a while before they once again shared the happy easygoing times of last evening. He saw her eying the breakfast table before dragging her gaze back to him. "I have a feeling breakfast will be cold by the time we get to it." And she was right. "Now, why are we contacting the police?"

"I believe I know who killed Symphony."

Her eyes widened and he saw she was slowly beginning to shake. She pulled the robe tighter.

"Who?"

"Ava Fletcher."

Kenny sat her down on his lap and explained to her how he'd seen the woman at the jewelry store and all of what Terry had revealed to him. She was completely stunned and horrified that someone seemingly so normal could do something so deranged and horrific. After she cursed and tried to wrap her head around all of it, she cried in his arms and Kenny Cavanaugh held his wife and did his best to absorb her pain and anger like he vowed to do.

He would take her on a proper honeymoon after she'd found some modicum of justice for her friend.

After she'd cried herself to sleep, he placed her in the bed and contacted a friend of his in the LAPD. Symphony's family and friends would finally get the closure they sought after so fiercely. He could not imagine the hell Kyle has been living. He also could not forget the lives Symphony positively made an impact on. His Ricco being one of them. Ricco was able to find refuge in a strange place after so much tragedy because of Symphony.

All the Phoenixes had loved her and had treated her like family. She'd made a positive influence on the neighborhood in Boston by donating food to the homeless shelters, providing internships for high school students, and offering scholarships and free tuition to the college students who worked for her. Symphony had not only left behind a bakery, she'd fostered and left behind a legacy.

Chapter 35

Five months passed and the pain of losing her friend had not lessened. Ricco and Kenny were tucked away in a cabin on one of the Great Lakes, but she couldn't remember which. All she knew was that wherever they were, it was freezing. Even with the temperatures below freezing, she insisted on sitting on the wraparound porch. She was wrapped in a warm quilt, there was a fire going, and Kenny was making his special hot chocolate inside.

Even though Ricco still missed her friend and boss, she did find a bit of comfort and peace knowing that the killer was found. Just a week ago Ava Fletcher was found guilty of first degree murder and was sentenced to life in prison.

After Terry called the detective handling the case and told him of Ava's obsession with Symphony along with what Kenny had told him about seeing her in California, they finally got a warrant to search her apartment. The police questioned Terry about why he hadn't spoken of it sooner, but just like everyone else, no one would have suspected her of such an act. No one really cared for the woman, but that wasn't enough to accuse her of murder. It wasn't until he was forced to think about the timing of the breakup and Symphony's death, as well as her sudden disappearance at work that he could see the connection.

The police found her gun wrapped in a towel in a shoe box. The gun was tested and discovered to be the murder weapon. She was found at the window of Barron Yaeger's, questioned, and confessed to killing Symphony as well as setting the fire in the trash can next to the bakery. She figured she was the reason Terry broke up with her. Ava was convinced that Terry was still in love with Symphony which hindered him from wanting to marry her. She probably wasn't too far from the truth. Everyone knew Terry still loved Symphony, but he had been resigned that she had moved on with her life and was determined to do the same.

Ricco and Kenny had been at the trial to support Kyle and his family. He, of course, was still angry and heartbroken, but was finding his strength in raising his daughter. He and Kenny's friendship gained strength and they had even spoken of going on a golf trip when the spring rolled around again.

Ricco still worried about what, if anything, he would do with the business. Sales were stronger than ever and the brand was gaining momentum even without broad advertisement. She loved her job and the Symphony's brand and would hate for him to sell or dissolve the company. It was something she'd spoken with Kenny about often. He always reassured her that things would work out. She never voiced it to him, but she wasn't so sure about that.

Another thing or person she didn't have to worry about was Ye-Jun Pak. The man who'd pretended to be a firefighter. He had been sent to Japan because the entire espionage operation had been discovered. Because the crimes were of a sensitive nature, there was not much more information shared with the U.S. government beyond what Cliff was able to find out. It was all classified. Cliff did discover that Pak was after Ricco because the information her parents had unknowingly retrieved from China, involved his grandfather somehow and implicated him in treason. Ricco and Kenny figured that was probably the true reason he did not return to China. He was most likely exiled. Ricco was a target because they had not known what information she may have discovered.

Ricco did take solace in finding out that her parents' murderers were captured along with all the people running the software company. Cliff had been instrumental in obtaining that information as well. She wondered if the innocent people, like her parents had been, were arrested as well. She figured she would never know. It made her sad thinking that many people had been extorted into participating in crimes, even if they'd discovered what was really going on.

"Here you are, baby." He handed her a huge mug. "Extra marshmallows, just like you like them."

The cup was a welcomed warmth. She blew at it and gingerly took a sip. "Perfect. Just like you." He leaned down, careful not to spill his own cup and kissed her soundly.

"Mmm. I love the taste of marshmallows off your lips. I will keep that in mind for future endeavors." He winked at her.

She rolled her eyes, loving how playful he was when they were on their own. He had been especially playful since they'd arrived at the cabin.

She looked out at the night. "Feels like a storm is coming. Everything feels so electric."

"My weather app says there's a strong chance of sleet and snow."

"Maybe we can get snowed in for a month." They'd both been so busy lately that they really hadn't gotten a chance to take a proper honeymoon.

He looked at her and cocked his head to the side. Something she noticed he did when he was concerned. "We haven't been spending enough time together, have we?"

"Is it ever enough?"

"Perfect answer, Mrs. Cavanaugh."

"Is there a proposal on the table, Mr. Cavanaugh?"

"I propose we stay until well after the new year."

Was he serious? She was supposed to be back right after Christmas, then realized, the staff could handle it. Kenny was rubbing off on her. He worked from home as often as he could and she found that she was working on the books for all the businesses more than being in the shop right now, so she could very well do that from anywhere as well.

"I accept your proposal, sir."

They sat in silence for a while, the fire warming them and lighting their faces in the darkness. Her mind brought her back to Symphony. Ricco's parents had been so loving, she could not imagine Symphony's life where her parents were so neglectful.

"You know, I'm really surprised that Symphony's parents didn't show up for the funeral or the trial."

"Didn't you know?"

"Know what?"

"They are both in prison."

"For what?"

"Real estate fraud and theft. Probably a bunch of other charges like trespassing and whatever goes along with that."

"Ok, now start from the beginning."

Stunned, Ricco listened to Kenny, and the lengths Symphony's parents had gone to get their hands on her property and money. They'd conned a couple into thinking Symphony's property in South Carolina was for sale, not realizing that if the property was to be sold, Dixon Phoenix would get first refusal. They didn't count on the couple being smart enough to do a little investigating on their own. They'd contacted law enforcement about what they suspected, the police set up a sting, and arrested Symphony's parents at the scene. The father was already on probation and the mother had been in jail countless times for drugs and prostitution.

"Prostitution?" Ricco exclaimed.

"Apparently that's how she'd found her way to Boston. She'd borrowed money from her ex-husband to keep from being on the streets like that. He'd convinced her to go to Boston to extort money from Symphony. The mother had been questioned after the murder, because Kyle knew she was after the money Aunt Helen left Symphony."

"Do you hear yourself?" She asked. "This all sounds like an episode from CSI."

He gave a wry smile. "Not anything less exciting than the stories we could tell."

"I guess you're right."

The quiet rose around them again and they sat in silence mining their own thoughts and drinking hot chocolate. They both rocked. It was Kenny who broke the silence. "Oh yeah, Terry told me that Joshua and Alex are having a girl."

She smiled and wondered when she and Kenny would start a family. "Lord help them if the baby's anything like her momma."

"They said they're going to name her Symphony."

Her throat was too tight to speak at the moment. She simply shook her head in response.

"Hey." The single word was spoken in a gentle, hushed tone.

Her eyes found his as they were always wanting to do and she smiled. "Hey."

"I have some news about Symphony's and I don't know how you're going to take it."

That got her attention. Her mug stilled at her mouth and she sat up. Needing to fortify herself with chocolate before he spoke, she took a sip then asked, "What's the news?"

"You now own fifty-one percent of Symphony's." One hundred questions slammed against her skull all at once. For the life of her she couldn't put them in a cohesive order to ask one. She simply stared at him like he'd grown an extra head. "Kyle wanted to sell the bakeries out right and I convinced him to keep thirty-nine percent. I'm sure his grief is ruling him right now. Ian owns ten percent. Symphony made him a partner after she had the baby. It was her way of keeping him. I've talked to Ian. He is not interested in doing anything more than what he's doing now."

"So Symphony's is ours?" She finally found the words to ask.

"It is my gift to you, Naricco. Plus, now instead of picking up boxes of baked goods for the office, maybe I can convince you to put a little bakery kiosk in my lobby."

She'd gone from sleeping on the floor of a shed to flying in jets, getting married, and now owning her own bakery. And all because of this man. She got up, placed her mug on the table between them and snuggled in his lap. Her most favorite place in the world. "I love you, Kenny Cavanaugh. And yes, you can have a little kiosk in your lobby." She kissed him with all the fervor and love he was due. Settling into him, they both watched the night and listened to the crackle of the fire roaring next to them. Suddenly bolts of lightning lit the sky, with a spectacular show.

"Wow! I've heard about it, but I've never seen that during a winter storm. Brilliant, isn't it?" He exclaimed.

"That's you, you know?"

"What?"

"Winter lightning—unexpected and brilliant."

"You're wrong, sweetheart. *Together* we are winter lightning."

The End.